"You put me through hell for eighteen years!"

Carter said, furious. "You were the only woman I ever loved. You destroyed my life. You made me incapable of loving again."

"What do you think you did to me? If we could do it over again…" Bonnie Jean thrust her hands in front of her in a pleading gesture.

"But we can't. Nothing can change the past," he said.

Bonnie Jean stood before him, her eyes damp with tears. "All I ever wanted was you. I loved you so much."

"What about now?" he asked, moving toward her, slowly, cautiously.

Did she still breathe? Did her heart still beat? "Do you…want…a second chance?"

"I want you. The hottest, wildest thing I've ever known."

Dear Reader,

Sugar Hill was a book I had to write. This love story haunted me for over a year, begging to be told. Bonnie Jean and Carter made brief appearances in my first book, *Yankee Lover,* and became characters I couldn't forget. They were lovers torn apart by family prejudice and their own youthful foolishness, but they were never able to forgive—or forget—each other. It was Carter's family who broke Carter and Bonnie Jean up seventeen years earlier, and it is Carter's mother and uncle who plot to right that wrong and reunite the lovers when the book begins. The sexual attraction between them is still so strong that, despite their deep-rooted hostility, they are powerless to resist temptation. But because Bonnie Jean possesses a tragic secret, she fears Carter will never forgive her once he knows the truth.

Of all my books, *Sugar Hill* remains one of my favorites. It is a highly sensual, deeply emotional story that celebrates the joy of being given a second chance at love.

All the best,

Beverly Barton

BEVERLY BARTON
Sugar Hill

Silhouette Books

Published by Silhouette Books

America's Publisher of Contemporary Romance

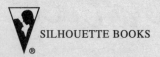

SILHOUETTE BOOKS

ISBN-13: 978-0-373-36151-9
ISBN-10:   0-373-36151-3

SUGAR HILL

BEVERLY BARTON

Beverly Barton has been in love with romance since her grandfather gave her an illustrated book of *Beauty and the Beast*. An avid reader since childhood, Beverly wrote her first book at the age of nine. After marriage to her own hero and the births of her daughter and son, Beverly chose to be a full-time homemaker, a.k.a. wife, mother, friend and volunteer. The author of more than fifty books, Beverly is a member of the Romance Writers of America and helped found the Heart of Dixie chapter in Alabama. She has won numerous awards and has made the Waldenbooks and *USA TODAY* bestseller lists.

To a very special lady
whose loyal and unselfish friendship
I treasure greatly,
Brenda Hall.

And a special thanks to Willie Wood,
for weekly doses of encouragement
and to Linda Howard,
who made me write this book.

Prologue

"**I** want an answer right now," Wheeler Yancey said, giving his sister a cold, determined look. "You're either with me or against me."

"For heaven's sakes, Brother, don't you think you're being a bit melodramatic?" Dorothea Moody lifted a delicate china espresso cup from the silver tray atop the Jacobean desk in Wheeler's study. "You're talking like we're on the verge of war and we have to take sides before the first battle."

Wheeler surveyed his younger sister with a critical eye, but couldn't find one single fault in her appearance. At sixty-two, Thea was as china-doll beautiful as she'd been at twenty. The few tiny laugh lines around her eyes and mouth, and the touch of silver in her black hair, were the only signs of age.

"This very well could turn into a war before we're

through.'' Wheeler gulped down the espresso and set his cup on the silver tray. ''Damn cups aren't big enough. Why you women have to be so dad-blame fancy I'll never know.''

''Adding little touches of civilization is one of the few ways to keep men like you from being totally barbaric.'' Dorothea sat down in a flame-print Queen Anne chair near the empty fireplace.

''Well, if you ask me, you've overcivilized that son of yours.'' Wheeler rested against the wall, leaning his arm on the Carrara marble mantel. ''He's forty, a widower with no children, and one of the most miserable human beings I've ever seen.''

Dorothea sipped her coffee, then balanced the cup and saucer in her open palm as she looked up at her brother. ''Of course he's unhappy. The woman he'd planned to marry just ran off to Florida and married another man. A Yankee stranger, of all things.''

''C.J. never would have married Laurel, and you damned well know it. They were like brother and sister.''

''Perhaps you're right.''

''You know I am.'' Wheeler turned around and looked out the long, narrow window facing the back lawn. Late-summer sunshine streamed through the open wooden shutters. ''C.J. hasn't been truly happy in eighteen years. Not since you persuaded me to help you play God with his life.''

Dorothea's lovely face paled, and her crystal blue eyes misted with tears. ''Carter spent eight years traveling the world as a newspaper correspondent. He loved that work. It's what he'd prepared himself to do.''

''If he loved it so much, why'd he come home ten years ago burnt-out and embittered?'' Wheeler kept his back to Dorothea, knowing if he saw her crying, he might not be able to bully her into helping him.

''He married a lovely girl. Kathie Lou was from one of the best families in Alabama.''

''He didn't love Kathie Lou any more than she loved him. It was practically an arranged marriage. Money married money.''

''Well, Carter truly enjoys editing the *Observer,* and you told me yourself that you could easily retire because he is so adept at running the family businesses.''

''Carter has turned into a straitlaced, stiff-shirted, boring snob.'' Wheeler turned around, willing himself to be strong. He needed his sister's help if he was going to save his nephew from spending the rest of his life a lonely, unhappy man.

Dorothea gasped, then quickly puckered her lips into a tight frown. With all the dignity she could muster, she swallowed her tears and faced the challenging stare in her brother's eyes. ''You think *she's* the answer, don't you?''

''I think she can make him happy.''

''How can you be so certain that they still care about each other? I mean, after all this time, surely they're not…not…in love.''

''I know my nephew, and I know Bonnie Jean. All you have to do is watch them when they're together, and you can just about see the sparks flying.''

"She probably still hates me," Dorothea said, her voice a mere whisper. "Not that I could blame her. If I help you get them together, who's to say she won't take Carter away from me completely?"

"We misjudged that girl once, Thea, let's not make the same mistake twice." Wheeler pointed his meaty index finger at his sister.

Dorothea stood, straightened the wrinkles in her pink linen slacks, and walked over to stand beside her brother. "I'm with you. I want to see Carter happy, but I'm afraid we might make matters worse."

"We interfered in their lives once with some pretty disastrous results, I admit." Wheeler placed an arm around Dorothea's shoulder and squeezed gently. "I guess it's only right that we should try to make amends."

She shook her head sadly. "After all this time?"

"Maybe it's not too late."

One

Carter Jackson Moody IV parked his white Mercedes in front of the old Victorian house and stepped out, straightening to his full six-foot-two height. He adjusted his aviator sunglasses, then scanned the front yard and the porch. *Where the hell is she?* he wondered. He knew she was here. The fire-engine red '59 Cadillac, blocking half the drive, announced her presence.

He eyed the overgrown brick walkway leading to the front porch. Grass and weeds grew knee-high all over the yard, untrimmed bushes dotted the landscape, and a scattering of broken tree limbs littered the ground.

Stepping carefully to avoid scarring his Italian leather shoes, Carter made his way to the porch. He eased one foot up, testing the sturdiness of the wooden structure. When it didn't give way, he stepped up and walked to the open front door. He started to call out to her, but stopped dead still when he looked into the dusty foyer.

A shapely rear end, clad in tight cutoff jeans, greeted his line of vision. Long, long tanned legs were bent in a semisquat as she reached down and ran her fingers over the dusty pine floor.

His breathing quickened, his heartbeat accelerated, and he felt a tightening in the lower part of his body. Damn her, he thought. Why did she have to look so good? A thirty-six-year-old woman shouldn't have such a sexy body, and heaven help him, he'd always thought Bonnie Jean had the sexiest body he'd ever seen.

He watched, fascinated by the way her long pale hair curled about her face, the ends of her loose ponytail caressing her neck. He wished he had his hands around her neck. The only thing he didn't know was whether he'd rather strangle her or kiss her.

She stood up, her back still to him, and dusted off her hands on her hips. Her hips were round and utterly feminine, and her waist was so tiny he was sure he could encompass it with both hands. He remembered a time when he had.

Pushing the memories aside, he stepped over the threshold and entered the foyer. He paused to wipe away the perspiration from his forehead. It was damn hot for early September, even in Alabama. The smell of an old house, long ago boarded up and unused, assailed him the moment he moved forward. He forced himself to stop staring at Bonnie Jean's tempting body, and looked around the cobweb-infested room.

The enormous foyer retained a vestige of its former glory. Although the silk flowered wallpaper was torn and discolored, and the heart-of-pine floors were nicked and scarred, the coal-converted fireplace appeared untouched by time. The pale green-and-cream marbled tiles surrounding the black metal insert and the carved oak mantel seemed to be in perfect shape.

This place had been built by his great-grandfather in the late 1880s, but had stood empty for the past forty years. His father had brought his mother to this house as a bride, and two years later, she had boarded it up and left, a pregnant young widow.

Why now, after all this time, had his mother agreed to his uncle's preposterous idea of allowing Bonnie Jean Harland to turn the house into a restaurant? He'd tried questioning his mother, but her answers had been so vague they'd left him more puzzled than ever. And all he could get out of his Uncle Wheeler was the suggestion that he get used to working with Ms. Harland now that she was a business associate.

Bonnie Jean brushed her dirty hands on her hips and took a deep breath. She knew C.J. was standing just inside the front door, and she knew exactly why he was here. Undoubtedly Wheeler had told him that they'd signed the contract this morning. She, Bonnie Jean Harland, the illegitimate daughter of Sally Vickers and widow of town bad boy Bubba Harland, was officially a business associate of Yancey-Moody Enterprises.

She didn't want to turn around and face C.J. No

doubt he'd be angry and probably accuse her of at least a dozen immoral deeds. Then they'd argue, and she'd wind up crying herself to sleep tonight. C.J. had the power to hurt her that no other human possessed.

It hadn't always been that way between them—the anger and pain. Once... *No, I won't remember!* she told herself. *What we had, ended long ago, and he'll never be able to forgive me.* In truth, she knew she had never been able to forgive him, either.

She realized she must look a mess, and not exactly ladylike. The one thing she tried very hard to do was always dress and act like a lady. She could just imagine what C.J. thought, seeing her like this. If only she'd put on slacks and a blouse instead of these old cutoffs and halter top. But when she'd dressed for comfort, she hadn't counted on running into C.J. Moody. *Please, Lord, don't let him think I look trampy.*

Bonnie Jean turned sideways, threw back her head and ran her fingers through her hair. She knew he was watching her, could feel his gaze touching her breasts. Her nipples hardened, and a tingle of excitement raced through her.

Gathering all her courage, she turned and faced him. "What are you doing here, C.J.?"

"I could ask you the same question."

"You mean you don't know?" She took a good look at him, and the sight of C.J., so close and yet so very far out of her reach, hurt her more than she wanted to admit.

"Why on earth would you agree to this business

deal knowing we'd have to work together?'' He walked into the foyer and looked around.

''The whole thing was Wheeler's idea, and a very good one if you ask me.'' She glared at him, irritated by the accusatory tone in his voice.

''What is this, a payoff for services rendered?'' C.J. regretted the words the moment they left his mouth. Her relationship with his uncle was nobody's business, least of all his. Wheeler and Bonnie Jean were both over twenty-one.

''You're really angry, aren't you?'' Bonnie Jean choked back the tears lodged in her throat. She refused to respond to his unjust taunt. If he'd intended to hurt her, he'd succeeded.

''I'm sorry, Bonnie Jean. I had no right—''

''No, you didn't, but having the right to say or do something has never stopped you before.''

''You know as well as I do that this business arrangement will never work out. We can't be in the same room for more than five minutes without being at each other's throats.''

Why did he have to look so good? she wondered. Big and tall and tan. And far more handsome than any man had a right to look. Pretty boy. She'd heard him called that quite a few times, and that's exactly what he was, even at forty, with faint lines around his crystal blue eyes and at the corners of his mouth. His once-black hair had turned salt-and-pepper, but it only added to his compelling good looks, as did the thick, dark mustache.

''I don't suppose you'd consider changing your

mind and letting Yancey-Moody Enterprises off the hook?'' he asked.

''Don't be silly. I'm a businesswoman, a pretty shrewd businesswoman if I do say so myself, and I've just signed a legally binding contract with Yancey-Moody.'' She watched him as he moved around in the foyer, his big, immaculately dressed body somewhat out of place in the dirty, ramshackle old mansion.

''What if I make you a better offer?'' He plunged his hands into the pockets of his tailored beige slacks.

''Why are you so afraid of me?'' she asked, and walked over to where he stood by the rickety staircase.

''I'm not afraid of you.'' He shook his head in a negative motion, but didn't raise his eyes to meet hers. ''You know what I think of you. Do you honestly want to be in business with a man who despises you?''

She clenched her hands at her sides, her long nails biting into her soft palms. *Don't let him get to you,* she warned herself. Even though he thought he had every reason to feel the way he did, his callous words hurt her deeply. No matter what he said, he *was* afraid of her, of the strong magnetism that had always been between them.

''I plan on turning this place into a fine restaurant.''

C.J. placed his big hand on the dusty banisters and gripped the top railing. ''I'd be willing to make it worth your while to reconsider.''

''No deal,'' she said, wondering if she wasn't ten

times a fool for agreeing to this business deal, no matter how successful she knew it would be.

"Name your price."

"This is ridiculous. You aren't going to get your way this time, Mr. Moody. Everything may have its price, but everyone doesn't."

"That's where you're wrong," he laughed. "And you should know better than anyone."

The urge to slap his face overwhelmed her, but she resisted the urge, knowing it would accomplish nothing but to further antagonize him. For the past eighteen years they had tried to avoid each other. For eight years, C.J. had traveled the world as a newspaper correspondent and for fourteen years Bonnie Jean had lived in Nashville. Of course, during the years they'd spent apart, each had married and been widowed. But four years ago, Bonnie Jean had come home, and though their paths had crossed occasionally, it wasn't until she became good friends with Laurel Drew, C.J.'s most recent girlfriend, that things began to change. They'd been thrown together often, and Bonnie Jean soon came to realize that the old desire C.J. had once felt for her was still there, only now it was mixed with contempt.

"You needn't remind me of what a naive idiot I was." She walked around in front of him and looked him squarely in the eye. "But I've grown up since then. I've changed. I'd never again be stupid enough to believe that you could ever love and trust me."

C.J. had seen that look of determination in her hazel eyes before, and he knew he was in for a fight. So be it. If she wanted a fight, he'd give her one.

He'd done everything within his power to stay away from her, but fate seemed to constantly throw them together. He didn't want to feel anything for Bonnie Jean Harland, but he did. After all this time, he still wanted her in a way he'd never wanted another woman.

Once, years ago, she'd been his, and she had become a slow poison in his system. No matter how hard he tried, he couldn't forget those wild and passionate days they'd shared the summer after his college graduation. He'd been a besotted fool, thinking a girl like Bonnie Jean actually knew anything about love. He'd learned the hard way that, like her mother, the only thing she really wanted from a man was his money.

"Do you realize how much it will cost to renovate this old place?" C.J. gripped the railing tightly and shook the staircase banisters. "It's falling apart. It'll take big bucks to turn it into anything resembling a first-class restaurant. A lot more than you spent on the Plantation downtown. Do you expect Yancey-Moody to foot the entire bill for this place?"

"I can assure you that between the locals and the tourist trade, there's no way we can lose money on this project." Bonnie Jean grabbed the railing and steadied it. She smiled at C.J., then looked down at his hand still resting on top of the banister. He removed his hand and took several steps up the staircase. She followed him, listening to the loud moaning from the stairs with each step he took. "Besides, I'm investing a great deal of my own capital in this place. I know the restaurant business."

"Heard you had a successful place in Nashville." C.J. kept walking up the stairs, not once looking back. "Ol' Bubba must've made some big bucks pickin' and singin' in Nashville."

"Yeah." She'd be damned if she'd tell C.J. that her husband had never made a living at anything, and had eventually turned to the bottle and a long line of one-night stands to ease the pain of his failures.

"Why'd you come back here after Bubba died? Why didn't you just stay on in Nashville?" C.J. walked into the upstairs hallway and ran into a clingy mass of cobwebs. He batted them away, and wiped them from his face.

"I wanted to come home." No matter how many painful memories existed on Sugar Hill, Bonnie Jean had needed to return, to find a place for herself in a town that had once looked down on her with such utter contempt.

"Why? There's nothing here for you."

When he started to enter the nearest room, Bonnie Jean stepped into the doorway in front of him. She placed her hands on her hips and glared at him. "I have friends here. And business associates." Her lips formed a satisfied smile.

"And memories?" Hell, he could kick himself for saying such an idiotic thing. He didn't want her to realize how often those memories haunted him.

"Yes. I have my memories, but they were as much a part of me when I lived in Nashville as they are here. Some things, a woman can never forget, no matter how hard she tries or how far she runs."

He turned around and walked toward another

empty room. Bonnie Jean followed him. He stomped on the floor and billows of dust flew into the air. She sneezed several times, and heard him laugh.

"Why did you do that?" she asked.

"Look." He pointed to where his foot had punctured the rotten wood. "Most of the floor in this room will have to be replaced."

"I know." She moved across the room and stood beside him, her body almost touching his. "That's why I'm here today. I'm checking things out to see how much work needs to be done."

"You should let the contractor check things out."

"I intend to do just that. But before Willis and Son gives the place a once-over, I wanted to inspect the house myself. I intend to be personally involved with every detail of the renovation."

"You're not going to hire Dewayne Willis. Yancey-Moody Enterprises has never used that no-good bum, and we're not going to start now."

"This is a Yancey-Moody-Harland project, and Dewayne happens to be an old friend of mine. Things have been rough for him the last few years, and he needs—"

C.J. laughed, his pale blue eyes sparkling with agitation. "Dewayne Willis can't stay sober long enough to keep his business going."

She jabbed her finger into C.J.'s chest several times. "He's been sober for almost a year now, but no one will give him a chance to prove he's changed."

C.J. grunted and shook his head with disgust. "And

you plan to risk our money giving him the chance? Not if I have anything to say about it.''

She jabbed his chest again to emphasize her anger and determination. C.J. glared down at her hand, and her gaze followed his. His chest rose and fell with the steady movement of his breathing. She tried to pull her hand away, but her fingers remained poised above his chest. She wanted to touch him. It would be so easy. All she had to do was lower her hand, palm open, and rest it against his silky red tie and tailored white shirt. ''I…I believe everyone deserves a… second chance.''

C.J. couldn't take his eyes off her hand. If she lowered it just a fraction, she'd be touching him. The steady punch of her fingernails against his chest had amused him until he realized he was becoming aroused by her nearness, by the slight touch of her body against his.

God, he hated that she still had so much power over him. He wasn't an emotional man, except around her. He was always in control of himself, his emotions, his every action. When he'd returned to Tuscumbia ten years ago, he had set goals for himself, and he'd achieved almost all of them. After the savage atrocities he'd witnessed as an overseas correspondent, he'd sworn that, if he ever got home in one piece, he'd revert back to the slow and easy life-style for which the old south was famous. His years in Southeast Asia and the Middle East had taught him a valuable lesson. After he'd seen a good friend, a fellow correspondent, blown to bits before his very eyes, he'd come home to Alabama, to a way of life that promised peace and stability. He wanted the strength and security of generations of breeding and culture. He needed the proud heritage from which he'd come. He returned home, determined to become the Southern gentleman his mother had always wanted him to be. And that's what he was, but Bonnie Jean undermined his life-style. She reminded him of the carefree young hellion he'd been all those years ago when he'd dared to fall in love with the town whore's illegitimate daughter.

C.J. turned around and walked out of the room. Bonnie Jean stood and watched as he went out into the hall and back down the stairs.

"Don't you walk away from me, Carter Jackson Moody! We're not through talking, not by a long shot." She raced out of the room and followed him down the stairs.

He'd known she wanted to touch him, and he'd run. The desire he felt for her frightened him. He'd gone halfway around the world trying to escape the memory of her betrayal. He'd married another woman, and every time he'd touched his wife he'd thought of Bonnie Jean.

She caught up with him at the open front door and grabbed him by the arm. He stopped immediately, but didn't turn around. He stood silently, his body rigid.

"I'm going to hire Willis and Son," she said, her voice deceptively soft and silky.

"Fine. You do that." He jerked away from her hold and stepped outside to the front porch.

"Just give me a chance, will you?"

He took one step down toward the yard, then stopped. "You've sweet-talked my uncle into this deal and now we're stuck with it, but I don't have to work with you. If Wheeler Yancey is so damned determined for you to be part of this project, then he can supervise."

"Fine with me!"

"Then there's no reason for us to have to see each other again, is there?"

His superior attitude prompted her to yell after him, "I'm going to call this place Sugar Hill." She smiled when she saw his big body stiffen. She knew that comment had gotten his attention.

He swung around and stepped back onto the porch, his pale blue eyes boring into her. "What?"

"I think it'll be very appropriate, don't you?"

"Are you crazy?"

She laughed, amused by the stricken look on his face. "I thought you might like the idea."

"Well, I don't." He moved toward her and grabbed her by the shoulders, his fingers biting into her soft flesh.

"This place could be a new beginning for me." She wanted a new beginning, the chance to prove to the whole town that she was more than white trash from the wrong side of the tracks.

He felt like shaking her until her teeth rattled. Why couldn't she do things the way any normal woman would? he asked himself. Stupid question. Because Bonnie Jean Harland wasn't like any other woman on earth. She was unique. "I don't want a new beginning. I like my life just the way it is." He tightened his hold on her.

"Let go. You're hurting me," she said, wiggling.

He loosened his grip on her shoulders, but didn't let go. He looked into her green cat eyes, eyes the color of gold-flecked jade. She'd told him to release her, but her eyes spoke another language—one that said, *"Never let me go."*

His gaze traveled down her small, tip-tilted nose to her full, pouty lips, and he felt himself sway toward her. If he kissed her, her mouth would be soft and warm and sweet. Over the years he'd experienced quite a few erotic dreams about her mouth.

He stared at her neck and then her breasts. Watching a trickle of sweat nestled in the hollow of her throat, he had the urge to taste its saltiness with his tongue. The drop of perspiration moved slowly down onto her chest and disappeared into the vee of her knit top, and he wished his gaze could follow.

His body tightened, and he hated himself for allowing her to have that effect on him. He looked at her face, but regretted the move when he saw her smile. *She knows I want her, dammit!*

Just as he started to release her, he noticed a smudge of dirt on her cheek and instinctively reached out to brush it away. The moment his fingers touched the satiny surface of her face, his hand froze.

He looked at her. She looked at him.

"Do you enjoy doing this to us?" he asked, his voice a ragged whisper.

She licked her lips like a hungry cat would before devouring a bowl of fresh cream, but she didn't say a word.

"Stay away from me, Bonnie Jean, or you'll regret

it.'' He jerked his hand back, but continued to glare at her.

"What I regret is that your stubborn pride is ruining any chance we might have of cooperating on this venture." She reached out and touched him, running the tip of one finger across his thick mustache. "Don't you know that I regret the past as much as you do?"

C.J. swallowed hard, closed his eyes, and took a deep breath. "Bonnie—"

They both heard the sound of a car in the drive, and turned around just in time to see Wheeler Yancey step out of his new Corvette.

Wheeler, a tall, robust man with dark blue eyes and thinning gray hair, wore jeans, a plaid work shirt and snakeskin boots.

"It's hotter 'n blue blazes for this time of year," Wheeler said as he removed his "Roll Tide" ball cap and wiped the sweat from his forehead.

Bonnie Jean sighed deeply. She didn't know whether to be relieved or distressed by the interruption. "Come on up here and get out of the sun," she said, taking several steps away from C.J.

"What are you doing here, boy?" Wheeler asked his nephew.

C.J. eyed the older man with a mixture of amusement and irritation. "I don't know what sort of game you're playing, but you can count me out. I have no intention of being part of this." C.J. spread his arm in a semicircle as he scanned the ramshackle house.

"Tarnation, boy, there's no need for you to be so bullheaded. Bonnie Jean's got her heart set on fixing

this old place up and turning it into a fine restaurant.''
Wheeler stepped up on the porch next to Bonnie Jean,
bent down and kissed her on the cheek.

"I can't believe Mother actually agreed to this lu-
dicrous idea." C.J. walked down the steps and to his
car. He turned around just before getting into his Mercedes. "Do me a favor, will you, Uncle Wheeler?
From now on check with me before you put Yancey-
Moody Enterprises' money into some harebrained
scheme.''

"This is no harebrained scheme. This place'll be a
gold mine. Bonnie Jean knows the restaurant business," Wheeler said. "Besides, it'll do you good to
take time off from playing newspaper editor and get
more involved in Yancey-Moody Enterprises. After
all, I might want to retire in a few years.''

"I'm not going to work with her." C.J. looked directly at his uncle, ignoring Bonnie Jean as if she
weren't even there. "If you want someone to oversee
this project, you'll have to do it." C.J. slid into the
front seat, started the engine and drove away. Swirls
of red-clay dust ascended into the air and floated toward the house. Bonnie Jean coughed several times
and fanned her hand around in front of her face.

"Gave you a pretty hard time, didn't he?" Wheeler
asked, placing an arm around Bonnie Jean's shoulders.

"When doesn't he?"

"If he gets any more rigid, he's going to break
clean in two. That boy's coiled tighter than a spring.''

"He's gotten worse since Laurel ran off to Saint
Augustine with John Mason.''

"Oh, she dented his pride a bit. The whole town had them pegged as the ideal couple, but he wasn't any more in love with Laurel than I was."

"I don't know if C.J. is capable of love. Laurel hurt him more by denting his pride than she ever could have by breaking his heart, because he doesn't have a heart."

Wheeler hugged her close to his side as they walked through the open front door. "Well, gal, there was a time when that boy had a heart, and he gave it to you."

"That was a lifetime ago. We're two different people now." She knew she wasn't the same insecure teenager she'd been eighteen years ago when she'd allowed Dorothea Moody and her own mother to almost destroy her life.

"True. But I think you'll be even better for each other now that you've matured. Working together should give y'all a chance to see if there's something left between the two of you."

"He's not going to work with me on this project," Bonnie Jean said as they sat down on the bottom step. "He disapproves of the whole thing and said you'd have to supervise the project."

"That's what he thinks," Wheeler laughed.

"Wheeler Yancey, you've been a good friend to me, and I appreciate everything you've done, but nothing is going to change the way C.J. feels about me or the way I feel about him." Bonnie Jean laid her head on Wheeler's big shoulder, and blinked the unshed tears from her eyes.

"He needs to be told the truth," Wheeler said, then

kissed her forehead. "That stubborn pride of his won't let him get past the fact that he thinks you took money from Dorothea to break up with him, and then ran off with Bubba."

"He'd never believe me. Not now. The only person he'd believe is his mother, and she's not likely to ever admit to her part in the whole thing."

"I'm not so sure about that. My sister isn't a stupid woman, even if she is a bit narrow-minded and something of a social bigot. She knows how unhappy C.J. is. And she wants to see him happy almost as badly as she wants grandchildren."

"You can't think she'd actually accept me in C.J.'s life, let alone want to see me as the mother of his children." Bonnie Jean's voice wavered ever so slightly, the thought of giving C.J. a child reviving old memories better left buried.

"Never say never." Wheeler's jovial attitude became somber as he looked at Bonnie Jean. "You stick to your guns and turn this place into the best restaurant in the Shoals. Don't let that stuffed-shirt nephew of mine slow you down. I'll take care of him."

"You're right. Absolutely right. Come on," she said, hopping up and pulling on his big hands. "Let me show you around the old Moody homestead and tell you about my plans for Bonnie Jean Harland's classy new restaurant, Sugar Hill."

"*Sugar Hill?*" With laughter rumbling in his burly chest, he released her hands and dropped back down on the steps. Wheeler looked up at her and saw the devilment twinkling in her eyes. "Sugar Hill," he repeated. His loud, masculine laughter filled the old house. "By golly, gal, that ought to do it."

Two

Bonnie Jean watched the sky as the soft pale glow of dawn spread through the darkness, daylight ever so slowly vanquishing the night. Clutching the railing, she leaned over the porch banisters and breathed in the sweet, fresh aroma of the September morning.

This house had been her home for the first eighteen years of her life, and when she'd left to go with Bubba to Nashville, she'd sworn she'd never come back. But time had a way of changing a person's mind as well as healing old wounds. She had considered selling the place after her mother died, but some sixth sense had told her to keep this small brick house on Sugar Hill.

She had returned to Tuscumbia almost four years ago, a few months after Bubba's death. She'd been so determined to prove to herself and the whole town

that she was a different person from the insecure, stig-
matized and very pregnant girl who'd run off with the
local bad boy.

Tuscumbia had changed a great deal over the years,
yet in some ways it hadn't changed at all. She'd made
new friends and renewed old acquaintances, but there
were still people who refused to accept Bonnie Jean,
people who couldn't see her as anything but Sally
Vickers' illegitimate daughter.

Carter Jackson Moody IV was one of those people.
The man thought the absolute worst of her. For eighteen years he'd believed she betrayed him, and in his
stern, unforgiving way, he was determined to ignore
the love they'd once known. Bonnie Jean almost en-
vied his ability to treat her with such vile contempt.
If only she could react to him in the same way. But
she couldn't. The only way she could handle her feelings for him was by deliberately goading him, joking
with him, and occasionally trying to cut him down to
size.

The sound of her laughter mingled with the song
of a morning bird as she remembered that, only a few
weeks ago, C.J. Moody had awakened on her living
room couch after coming to her home the night before. He'd been falling-down drunk. C.J. wasn't a
drinking man, and everyone knew he would walk a
mile out of his way in order to avoid Bonnie Jean
Harland.

But sometimes a man acted out of character, especially when he was losing the woman his mother
and the whole of Colbert County had chosen to be
his next wife. Bonnie Jean had known that Laurel

Drew and C.J. were totally wrong for each other. All you had to do was be around them for five minutes to see that they bored each other to tears. They couldn't generate one little spark between them.

And when that big, blond Yankee had shown up at the Keller Festival two months ago, Bonnie Jean had known Laurel Drew was lost to C.J. forever. So, when he'd come to her house late one night looking for his Uncle Wheeler, Bonnie Jean hadn't been surprised that C.J. had been ranting and raving about having fixed Laurel and her Yankee lover but good.

When C.J. passed out, Wheeler asked Bonnie Jean to let him sleep it off on her couch, and she had reluctantly agreed. But the moment he awoke and realized where he was, he'd had a fit. She knew the last place on earth he wanted to be was under her roof, and it had killed his soul, not to mention dented his pride, to find out he'd lost control of his emotions in front of her. Carter Jackson Moody IV never lost control…except with her.

When she'd come home to Tuscumbia four years ago to bury her husband alongside his kinfolk, Wheeler Yancey had attended the funeral and stayed on at the house hours afterward. He'd been the one to tell Bonnie Jean what a straitlaced stuffed shirt C.J. had become. If anyone had ever told her that wild and fun-loving C.J. Moody would have turned into a prig, she'd have laughed herself silly. But she'd come to realize that Carter Moody was no more the young man he'd been eighteen years ago than she was the same foolish young girl. Life had dealt them both some pretty rough blows, and it looked like they had a few more hurdles to overcome.

The chance to turn the old Moody home into a first-class restaurant was a challenge Wheeler Yancey had known she wouldn't be able to refuse, but Bonnie Jean didn't kid herself. That devious old man had an ulterior motive—he wanted her and C.J. to have a second chance. He'd even admitted as much when he'd come to her with the idea.

"Look, gal," Wheeler had said, "Dorothea and I made a big mistake busting you two up all those years ago. It's only right that we be the ones to figure out a way to get the two of you back together."

"I know you mean well, but I don't want a second chance with C.J. I don't trust him any more than he trusts me. I'll never risk letting him hurt me again."

"Gal, all that is behind you. Besides, most of it was mine and Thea's fault, and we both feel differently about you now. Thea's come to realize that you're the one person who could make C.J. happy."

"Even if Dorothea Moody would accept me as a part of her son's life, it's too late. I'd rather die than to ever again know the pain C.J. caused me."

"Things change. People change."

Wheeler Yancey had a way about him, Bonnie Jean thought. Once, years ago, she'd hated him, almost as much as she'd hated Dorothea. But she'd long since forgiven him, and he'd become one of her dearest friends over the past few years. She knew his motives for wanting to see C.J. and her together again weren't purely unselfish. He'd told her that, even if she had forgiven him, he'd never be able to forgive himself until he saw C.J. and her reunited.

Was it really possible for people to get a second chance? Bonnie Jean wondered. Were there people brave enough to try again and not fear making the same mistakes? If only she hadn't been so naive eighteen years ago, so insecure, so totally lacking in self-confidence, she would never have given up a life with C.J., no matter how difficult it would have been for them to gain the town's acceptance. She would have stayed and fought for the man she loved, fought everyone's prejudice and distrust, even C.J.'s. But now it was too late.

She had loved him so much, so deeply and completely, with all the passionate intensity of first love. But his love had turned to hatred because his mother and hers had schemed together and had plotted the destruction of their children's relationship. If only he'd trusted her. If only he'd believed her when she'd tried to explain. Bonnie Jean hadn't had the self-confidence to fight for their love. She had always known she wasn't good enough for him, and she'd allowed her own mother to convince her that, without her, C.J. could have the kind of life he'd been born for—a life with a woman worthy of him.

Pain swelled inside of Bonnie Jean, gripping her heart, tightening her throat, smothering her. She'd been such a gullible little fool! But she wasn't an insecure girl any longer. She was a smart, tough businesswoman. So why, dear God, after all this time, did the memories still hurt her so? Was it possible that she still loved C.J. Moody?

* * *

Carter Jackson Moody IV gave himself a quick once-over in the bathroom mirror, running his hand over his smoothly shaved chin. He stepped into his adjoining bedroom, picked up his cream linen jacket and slipped his arms into the sleeves.

He dreaded facing his uncle at the breakfast table this morning. The old man was as stubborn as a mule, and he'd fight tooth and nail to make C.J. work on the restaurant project with Bonnie Jean Harland. He didn't know why his uncle was so determined to throw him into harm's way. Wheeler knew, better than anyone, why he couldn't stand being in the same room with that woman. His uncle had helped him live through those horrible days right after Bonnie Jean had ripped his heart out, those dark, miserable days when he'd had to accept the fact that the girl he loved had never loved him. All she'd ever wanted was money. At first, when his mother had told him that Bonnie Jean had offered to end their relationship for ten thousand dollars, Carter had laughed in Dorothea Moody's face. He'd been so sure of himself, of Bonnie Jean, and so confident in the passionate love they shared.

Hell, he'd been a fool. And he'd found out just how big a fool the night he'd caught her in Bubba Harland's arms. God, he'd never forget that night. And he'd tried. He'd gone halfway around the world, covering the news in every hellhole known to mankind. He'd tried to find solace with other women, but those relationships failed. Then he'd come home, married a suitable woman whom he didn't love, and become a Southern gentleman. But he'd never been able to forget that night, and heaven help him, after all this time, he could still remember what it felt like to love Bonnie Jean Harland.

C.J. walked into the hallway. His home was beautiful, but he'd never truly appreciated the splendor of the three-story antebellum mansion until he'd lived away from Alabama, away from the United States. Those years as a foreign correspondent had taught him to appreciate the life-style he'd always taken for granted.

He walked down the back staircase and entered the huge, sunny kitchen. The smell of smoked ham and red-eye gravy made his mouth water. He watched while Lula Mae lifted a pan of golden brown biscuits from the oven and slid them onto a platter.

"Your mama's already had her breakfast," the tall, white-haired housekeeper said. "She's complaining about you running late."

"Oh, Mother's always complaining about something." C.J. swiped a biscuit off the platter as he followed Lula Mae into the dining room.

"I'll bring your plate right in," Lula Mae said. "You want some of my pear preserves to go on these biscuits?"

Seating himself beside his mother, C.J. leaned over and kissed her lightly rouged cheek. "Open up a fresh jar, Lula Mae," C.J. said. "And I want some extra gravy."

"Good morning, dear," Dorothea said.

"You're looking lovely, as usual." C.J. scanned the room, puzzled by his uncle's absence. "Where's Uncle Wheeler? He hasn't already left, has he?"

"Well, as a matter of fact, he has." Dorothea wiped the corner of her mouth with a white linen napkin.

C.J. checked the time on his gold Rolex. "It's only ten after eight. He never leaves this early."

"He didn't go into town, dear." Dorothea reached for her coffee cup.

"Where did he go?" C.J. saw the slight tremor in his mother's hand, the hesitation in her clear, blue eyes. Something was going on, and he knew whatever it was, he wasn't going to like it.

"Well, he took Mrs. Jeffreys away on a little vacation." Dorothea smiled, then took a dainty sip from her Wedgewood cup.

"He *what?*"

"He took Mrs. Jeffreys—"

"Who the hell is Mrs. Jeffreys?"

"There's no need for you to use such foul language so early in the morning, Carter."

"Who is Mrs. Jeffreys, and why would Uncle Wheeler take her on a little vacation?"

"She's his latest…er…his current lady friend."

"I thought Bonnie Jean Harland held that position."

Dorothea gasped, and with trembling fingers set her cup back in its saucer. "Don't be ridiculous. You couldn't possibly have thought such a thing."

"Why not? Ever since she moved back here, they've been seen everywhere together. Most folks around here certainly think they're a couple." C.J. had never had the guts to ask his uncle exactly what his relationship was with Bonnie Jean. He'd been too afraid the answer would have twisted the knife that woman had left buried in his heart eighteen years ago.

"Well, I can assure you that the affection your uncle feels for Ms. Harland is quite fatherly."

"And just how do you know?" C.J. eyed his mother suspiciously.

"We've discussed Ms. Harland."

That revelation certainly surprised C.J. His mother had never been subtle in her dislike of Bonnie Jean, nor in her attempts to find him another suitable mate since Kathie Lou's death five years ago. "Why?"

"Why what?" Dorothea asked.

"Why would you and Uncle Wheeler discuss Bonnie Jean?"

"Well, Wheeler needed my approval before he could do anything with your father's old home."

"After all these years, you finally decided that it was time to reopen the old place. And not only reopen it, but give it to Bonnie Jean Vickers Harland to turn into a restaurant. Why, Mother?"

Dorothea Moody's cheeks flushed slightly, brightening the tint of her carefully applied blush. "Wheeler convinced me that it would be an excellent investment. After all, Ms. Harland owned a highly successful restaurant in Nashville, and The Plantation is one of the—"

"Mother!" He knew when his mother was fabricating one of her little white lies.

"Wheeler said to inform you that you'd have to take over things while he's away," Dorothea said as she turned to face her son. "He said to be sure to set up a meeting with Ms. Harland sometime today."

"Damn!"

"Whatever is the matter with you?"

"Are you in on this, too?"

"Carter, I think you should go back to bed and get up on the right side this time. You aren't making any sense." Dorothea laid her napkin beside her empty breakfast plate and stood up. "I have some correspondence to take care of, and then I'm meeting Polly Drew to work on plans for this year's antique auction at the country club."

"How long are Uncle Wheeler and Mrs. Jeffreys going to be gone?"

"He said he wasn't sure, but he did say he knew it would be at least three weeks." Dorothea patted her son on the shoulder. "Of course, he has every confidence in your ability to handle things in his absence."

"I'll just bet he does."

Long after his mother had gone up to her sitting room and Lula Mae had served his breakfast, C.J. sat alone at the dining room table thinking about what he was going to have to do. Whether he liked it or not, he would have to work with Bonnie Jean. Hell, why not? Maybe it was time he proved to himself that he was over her. He'd carried around so much hate for so long, it had begun to eat at his insides like a strong acid. Uncle Wheeler had told him he was turning into a bitter old man at the age of forty.

Maybe, just maybe, this was the opportunity to rid himself of the one thing that had obsessed him, the one person who had haunted his life and the one emotion that had robbed him of his ability to be happy.

With long, purposeful strides he made his way to the study. He checked the telephone directory for the number, punched out the digits and waited.

"The Plantation Restaurant, good morning," Bonnie Jean said.

"This is Carter Moody. I need to see you today."

"Well, hi there, C.J. How're you doing?"

"Can you be in my office at ten?"

"No."

"What time would be convenient for you?" he asked, trying, with great difficulty, to remain calm.

"I can't get away from The Plantation all day," she replied. "If you want to talk to me, you'll have to come here."

"That's out of the question."

"We'll have to make it another time then. Bye."

The dial tone rang in his ears like a taunting voice. Damnation, she'd hung up on him. How dare she! Oh, she dared all right. Bonnie Jean Harland had dared do a lot worse to him.

C.J. entered The Plantation restaurant through the back door. After spending four hours trying to talk himself out of doing anything foolish, he'd decided to confront Bonnie Jean.

"What are you doing in my kitchen, Mr. Moody?" the fat, gray-haired cook asked as she wiped her fleshy hands on her apron. "Customers are supposed to use the front entrance."

A slender young brunette wearing a beige waitress uniform stopped placing dishes on a serving tray and walked over to where C.J. stood near the huge refrigerator. "You here to see Bonnie Jean?"

"Where is she?" he asked, wondering why the young woman looked familiar.

"She's out in the restaurant with some customers."

"Would you please tell her I'd like to talk to her?" C.J. straightened his already-straight tie, and leaned back against the wall.

"Sure. But you could just go out there and talk to her."

"I'd rather see her in private." He didn't want half the town speculating on why he'd come to see Bonnie Jean.

C.J. watched the cook stirring what smelled like stew in an enormous metal pot atop the stove. She asked about his mother, about Wheeler and about the newspaper. She inquired about his health, his financial affairs and his nonexistent love life. Waitresses came in and out, each one giving him the once-over and giggling like a silly little girl. By the time the brunette waitress returned, he felt as if he'd taken part in the Spanish Inquisition.

"Bonnie Jean said for you to come on out there, and she'd be with you in a minute," the waitress said.

"But I didn't..." What's the use? he thought. Bonnie Jean knew why he wanted to see her, and the reason he was trying to keep the meeting private. Which, of course, was totally ridiculous since the waitresses were buzzing with the news that Carter Moody was waiting in the kitchen to see their boss.

He walked across the kitchen and through the swinging doors leading into the restaurant. He stood to the side, trying to be as discreet as possible, and spotted Bonnie Jean halfway across the restaurant. Her hazel eyes sparkled as she talked to a table of male customers.

The men were acquaintances of his, one an old college buddy. All three seemed to be enjoying not only their noon meal, but the company of the restaurant's owner. He could hear Bonnie Jean's husky laughter and see the way the men reacted to her warm smile. She was the type of woman a man had certain dreams about, and no doubt all three of those salivating idiots would have pleasant slumbers tonight.

When she glanced his way, he nodded his head, motioning for her to come to him. Damn, but she looked good. Her silvery blond hair was piled atop her head and secured with a thick gold barrette. Soft curls clung to her forehead and caressed her earlobes. She turned to him, smiled and waved, and all three men turned to look in his direction.

"Looks like Carter's trying to get your attention," Oliver Merritt said, and his two luncheon companions laughed.

"Does, doesn't it?" Bonnie Jean said. "You boys excuse me, and I'll go see what C.J. wants. Enjoy your meal, and I'll see you tomorrow." She swung around, swaying her hips, and walked through the crowded restaurant toward the stone-faced man standing by the kitchen door.

She knew he wasn't happy because she'd made him come to her. A man like C.J. was used to people doing his bidding. He was the one usually in charge— the always-reserved, controlled Mr. Moody. No doubt he'd found out that Wheeler had taken Mrs. Jeffreys to Saint Croix. That's the reason he was standing there glaring at her with such a determined look in his eyes.

Oh, he was angry! *Serves him right,* she thought. Coming in the back door as if he were ashamed to be seen with her. Well, he'd just have to get over it. They would be spending a lot of time together in the next few months, and she intended to demand the respect and consideration he would give any other business associate.

"Well, hello, C.J. What brings you here?" she asked, standing directly in front of him and smiling.

"You know damned well why I'm here," he said, his voice an agitated whisper.

"Why don't we have lunch together and discuss the details?"

"I have no intention of having lunch with you." He raised his voice slightly, then glanced around the restaurant. The brunette waitress passed by them as she went into the kitchen. She paused, smiled at C.J., and shook her head. "Who is she?"

Bonnie Jean watched her sister-in-law go into the kitchen, then turned around and said, "That's Elaine."

C.J. looked puzzled. "Who?"

"Bubba's baby sister. She's a waitress here and the assistant manager. When I open Sugar Hill, she's going to take over here as manager."

"You aren't going to call that place Sugar Hill."

"Sure I am. But we can settle that later. For now we have more important things to discuss." She leaned up against him and batted her eyelashes. "Why won't you have lunch with me? Your old buddy Oliver asked me to join him and his friends."

C.J. balled his hands into fists and held them tensely at his sides. "Stop it, Bonnie Jean. People are staring at us."

"You didn't used to be so concerned about what people thought." There had been a time when he'd told her that nothing and no one mattered except the two of them. He hadn't cared that she was Sally Vickers' bastard.

He grabbed her by the elbow, tugging gently. "Let's go in the kitchen."

She jerked away and glared at him. "No."

"What do you mean *no?*"

"I'm not going to hide in the kitchen to prevent your embarrassment."

"Bonnie Jean," he warned.

She turned around and walked toward the front door to greet a newly arrived customer. She talked and smiled, putting on her best hostess face.

She moved about The Plantation, speaking with numerous patrons, making sure everyone was satisfied with their meal and the service. Occasionally she glanced toward the kitchen door. C.J. didn't move. He stood rigidly, his pale blue eyes watching her every move.

When she walked toward the cashier, she passed C.J. He called her name quietly, but she ignored him. He reached out and grabbed her arm, pulling her up against him, then knocked open the swinging door and dragged her into the kitchen. Once inside, he pushed her up against the wall.

"Just what do you think you're doing?" She took one deep breath after another, trying to control her anger.

He leaned into her, his hard chest pressing against her breasts. "I want to talk, and I don't want half of Tuscumbia listening to our conversation."

"Dammit, C.J., let me go."

"I asked you to meet me at my office, but you wouldn't. So I had to come here, but you refused to see me in private. You're playing games with me, and I don't like it."

She shoved against his chest, but didn't budge him. She beat against his shoulders and wiggled her body trying to escape. He captured her hands, pushed them above her head and held them against the wall.

"Whatever you and Uncle Wheeler are up to isn't going to work. You're not going to win," he said.

"This isn't a game. This is business," she said breathlessly. "Now let me go."

He looked at her. She looked at him. Still holding her arms above her head, he leaned down, his big body crushing her. She writhed beneath him, a tiny cry escaping her throat just before he lowered his head.

"No." That one word said so much. He knew he was going to kiss her, but couldn't stop himself. It was a kiss of anger and frustration, he told himself, not one of affection or desire.

"C.J.?" Her lips parted just as she closed her eyes. His lips touched hers. Tenderly, tentatively at first.

He grunted. She groaned. And he took her mouth with fierce passion. Their bodies trembled with the force of a hunger long denied. The kiss went on and on, his tongue thrusting inside her mouth, moving back and forth, wet and warm and possessive.

The cook cleared her throat. ''The delivery man's coming in the back door, folks. You might want to postpone this unless you'd like to put on a show for him.''

C.J. released her immediately. She dropped her arms to her sides.

''Never again.'' He growled the words as he walked out the back door, almost knocking down the delivery man.

''Never again,'' she whispered, and ran her tongue over her swollen lips.

Three

"Do you think he'll actually show up?" Elaine Harland asked.

"Oh, he'll show up. C.J.'s a man of honor. He'll fulfill the terms of my contract with Yancey-Moody Enterprises even if it kills him. And me, too." Bonnie Jean laughed, her deep-throated chuckle masking a mixture of pain and uncertainty.

Elaine looked around the dreary room that had once been the kitchen of the old Moody house. "I can't believe Dorothea Moody actually agreed to open this place up. I heard she had it boarded up just a few weeks after her husband died over forty years ago."

"I think Wheeler twisted her arm." Bonnie Jean raked one finger across the dusty wall, leaving a semi-clean line on the plaster surface.

"Are they playing matchmakers?"

Bonnie Jean knelt on one knee and examined the threadbare linoleum flooring. She picked at the cracked surface with the tips of her fingernails. "I wonder what condition the wooden floor beneath is going to be in when we get this stuff ripped up?"

"Don't change the subject on me," Elaine said, adjusting her shoulder bag. "I've only got a few minutes before my shift at The Plantation, but I'm not leaving until we talk."

"Why don't you go spend your last few minutes with that handsome fiancé of yours?"

"I'll kiss Nick goodbye before I leave. Now, about your love life…"

Bonnie Jean stood and walked toward the door leading out to a screened back porch. The screens hung precariously from rotted frames, the strong breeze flapping several back and forth. "I've never interfered in your love life."

"Oh yes you have. You kept me from making the worst mistake of my life with Toby Hendricks." Elaine stomped her foot. "We're going to talk about this whether you want to or not."

"There's nothing to talk about." Bonnie Jean walked over to a rusty metal lawn chair that had been placed against the corner wall. She fumbled with the jam box resting across the seat. She removed the tape, flipped it over and punched the Play button.

Elaine put her arm around her sister-in-law's shoulder, hugging her lightly. "You were in love with Carter Moody when you married Bubba, weren't you?"

"Yes." Bonnie Jean closed her eyes for a fraction of a second as the soft wail of an old Patsy Cline song drifted through the humid September air. Her mother had always had country music playing at their house, and Patsy Cline had always been Bonnie Jean's favorite. Music was one of the few pleasant memories she had of their house on Sugar Hill.

"I knew, even as a kid, that there was somebody else. Somebody special," Elaine said.

"I tried to be a good wife to Bubba."

"You were. I didn't mean to imply otherwise. It's just that once I got older, I realized that you and Bubba didn't…well, you didn't love each other. Not that way…and that's when I started wondering about the baby."

Bonnie Jean leaned against the rickety door frame. The wooden surface was hard and hot. She took a deep breath and willed herself not to cry. "You always were too smart."

"Your little girl was Carter Moody's child, wasn't she? That's why you married Bubba in such a hurry."

"Your brother and I had been buddies since we were children. We were two of a kind. A couple of tough kids from the wrong side of town. Bubba and I had an understanding. I needed a father for my baby, and he needed somebody to take care of his little sister when he was on the road with the band."

Bonnie Jean would never forget the day Bubba Harland had proposed to her. He'd been nineteen to her eighteen, a boy who'd been saddled with the responsibility of raising his ten-year-old sister. The town blue bloods had looked on Bubba with utter contempt because his father had been a bootlegger, and he was a long-haired boy playing guitar at the state-line honky-tonks. And even though Bubba had helped Sally Vickers destroy Bonnie Jean's relationship with C.J., she had agreed to marry him. He had offered her the chance to have and keep her baby, and she would have wed the devil in order to protect her child. Her marriage had lasted fourteen years, and it had been the second biggest mistake she'd ever made.

"After you lost Cara Jean, why didn't you get a divorce?"

"A bargain is a bargain. Besides, I owed Bubba, and I'd grown to love you dearly."

Elaine hugged Bonnie Jean, then released her. "Oh, honey, I know what hell my brother put you through with his drinking and womanizing and gambling."

"Bubba was an unhappy man. He wanted to make it big in country music and couldn't accept the fact that he never got his big break, not even in Nashville."

"Well, the big idiot ended his misery when he crashed his motorcycle, didn't he?" Moisture coated Elaine's dark eyes.

A tall, muscular young blond walked through the opening where a screen door had once been. His boyish good looks would attract attention wherever he went. Bonnie Jean smiled at him, then turned to watch the way her sister-in-law's eyes glazed over in adoration.

"We've got a job cut out for ourselves on this place," Nick Willis said. "A few more years of age and neglect and it wouldn't be worth the money to fix up."

"Well, fix it up is what I aim to do," Bonnie Jean said. "I have all the confidence in the world in my future brother-in-law's ability as a contractor."

"Yeah, well, I appreciate that, Bonnie Jean, and so does Dad. Not many folks are willing to give him work. I promise we'll do one hell of a job. I need to prove myself as much as Dad does, seeing as how this is my first real project since I went into business with the old man." Nick leaned over and kissed Elaine on the lips.

Elaine nudged closer to him. "I've got to go, honey. How about a hug?"

"You'll get filthy. I've been crawling underneath the house." He brushed dirt, cobwebs, and dried leaves off his shirt and jeans, then grabbed Elaine and gave her a tongue-thrusting kiss.

"Have you two no shame?" Bonnie Jean asked, deliberately frowning. "Whatever will the neighbors think?"

Elaine chuckled and shook her head. "There are no close neighbors. Besides, you never used to give a hoot what the neighbors thought. As a matter of fact—"

"You'd better go or you'll be late," Bonnie Jean said.

"You don't have anything to prove to anybody, Bonnie Jean. You're a real lady and a real woman. If a certain someone had a brain in his head, he'd realize that." Elaine turned and walked back into the house. She called out to Nick, "See you tonight, honey. Try to talk Bonnie Jean into a double date."

Bonnie Jean smiled at Nick and held up her index

finger in warning. Nick grinned a lopsided, irresistible grin. "She's a bossy little witch, but I love her," he said. "She's right, you know—"

"Hush! Don't you get started."

The sound of Elaine's car starting coincided with the sound of another car's arrival. Bonnie Jean looked down at her sporty digital watch and knew that C.J. had arrived exactly on time. Ten o'clock.

"That's probably Moody," Nick said.

"Yeah."

"I don't look forward to working with him. Dad says he's one tough dude, hard as nails and doesn't put up with mistakes of any kind."

"Yes. He's never been known to give anybody a second chance," Bonnie Jean said.

C.J. stood in the open doorway leading from the central hall into the kitchen. He could hear the deep murmur of a male voice and the crystal-clear echo of Bonnie Jean's laughter. A stab of jealousy sliced through his midsection. When he'd met Elaine Harland's car leaving just as he arrived, he had assumed Bonnie Jean would be waiting for him alone. He had envisioned the way she'd look at him with those big hungry eyes of hers. He'd prepared himself for the onslaught of desire she always ignited within him. He'd been so damned sure she'd start trying to seduce him the minute he set foot out of his car. The thought that she was out back with some man, laughing, enjoying herself, made him want to kick something. Preferably a certain lady's well-rounded behind.

He stepped into the kitchen just enough to see the

tall, good-looking *boy* with whom Bonnie Jean was flirting. Dammit all, he was too young for her. He didn't look a day over twenty-five.

The big, blond Adonis draped his arm around Bonnie Jean's shoulder and said something to her that made her laugh even harder. C.J. wanted to rush onto the back porch and pull the boy away from her. Instead he took several tentative steps forward, then froze when he saw Bonnie Jean lean over and kiss the boy on the cheek.

Good God, had the woman no shame? Had she stooped so low she was robbing the cradle? Well, not exactly the cradle, C.J. admitted. This muscle-bound young Romeo might be a few years Bonnie Jean's junior, but he sure as hell didn't look like a child.

"I already have other plans for tonight," Bonnie Jean said.

"Going somewhere with Wheeler Yancey?" Nick asked.

"Wheeler's in Saint Croix on vacation."

C.J. felt like a eavesdropper, but he didn't feel guilty enough to make his presence known. He simply stood quietly and listened.

"You're pretty fond of that old man, aren't you?" Nick reached down into the six-pack cooler next to the metal lawn chair and retrieved an icy cola. "Want one?" He nodded his head toward the cooler.

"Sure. An orange soda, please." She sat down on the dirty wooden floor and crossed her legs Indian style. "And turn the tape up a little so I can hear it when we go back inside."

"Your wish is my command," Nick said teasingly.

"Just what I like, an obedient man."

Nick handed her the orange drink and sat down beside her. "You're a knockout, Bonnie Jean. You know, you're too much woman not to have a man around."

C.J.'s whole body tightened. He could feel the blood pumping through his body, could hear the accelerated beat of his heart. No, the good-looking guy sitting beside Bonnie Jean was no child. It was obvious he was an aggressive male intent on seducing the woman he'd just referred to as a knockout. C.J. didn't like the idea one little bit. He couldn't stand the thought of her being with another man. All the years she'd been married to Bubba Harland, C.J. had fought the torment of imagining her sharing the man's bed every night. What had hurt him the most was when Oliver Merritt's sister Barbara had casually mentioned that Bonnie Jean and Bubba had had a child.

C.J. stood so stiffly, so unmoving, that his whole body began to ache. Suddenly he let out a long breath, realizing he'd been holding it, waiting to hear Bonnie Jean's response to her young would-be lover's come-on.

"You're sweet to be concerned about me, Nick." Bonnie Jean put her hand on top of Nick's and squeezed gently.

When C.J. saw the two of them exchanging sickeningly sweet smiles, it was all he could do to keep from turning around and walking to his car and driving away. Being here was the most ridiculous thing he'd ever done. But, by God, he had no intention of reneging on a business deal with that platinum-haired she-devil. Even if it killed him. Even if it killed both of them.

"This thing you've got going with Wheeler Yancey…well…what I'm trying to say is, just how serious is it? I mean, are you going to marry him or something?" Nick asked.

C.J. didn't know what he'd expected her reply to be, but it certainly wasn't the torrent of earsplitting giggles that erupted from Bonnie Jean. He didn't know how to react. Bonnie Jean marry his Uncle Wheeler? The thought had never crossed his mind. In fact, he had dismissed the gossip about Bonnie Jean and his uncle long before his mother assured him that the two were just good friends.

"God A'mighty, Bonnie Jean. What did I say?" Nick looked at her as if he thought she'd lost her mind.

"Nothing," she giggled. "Oh, Nick—" she giggled again. Then she noted how he was staring at her, and she tried to restrain her outburst. "I'm sorry. I can't explain why I found the idea of marriage to Wheeler so funny. Let's just say that there isn't a snowball's chance in hell that Wheeler Yancey will become my husband."

"He sure acts like he cares about you."

"He does." Bonnie Jean sobered, her laughter softening to a sigh. She smiled. "And I've become awfully fond of him over the last few years. He thinks he owes me something, and he's determined to try to repay me."

It was hearing the statement about Wheeler owing

Bonnie Jean that triggered C.J. into action. He turned to go back down the hallway and caught the toe of his boot on a piece of ripped linoleum. He felt himself about to fall, splayed his hands open, and caught himself against the wall. His hands making contact with the plaster surface created a small smacking sound. He stiffened, wondering if he had given away his presence.

"C.J., is that you?" Bonnie Jean called out. "We're out here on the back porch."

Hell, he was in no mood to face that hussy. If her *boyfriend* left him alone with her, he might wind up saying or doing something he'd regret. Jealousy was one of the primitive emotions Bonnie Jean always brought out in him. After all this time, the memory of seeing her with Bubba Harland was as vivid and painful as it had been the night it happened.

C.J. marched through the kitchen and onto the back porch. "I hope I'm not intruding," he said.

Bonnie Jean looked up at him and smiled. "What are you shouting about?"

C.J. snarled. He felt the maddening heat suffuse his face and knew Bonnie Jean realized he was close to losing control. Dammit, why did this woman, and no other, have such a strong effect on him? He looked down at his watch. "It's ten. I said I'd be here at ten. If I'm interrupting something, I can leave and come back later." He wasn't going anywhere. If she intended to seduce this boy, she'd have to do it another time because he wasn't about to let anyone touch her right now. Not unless he did, and that would be to strangle her.

"You're not interrupting a thing," Bonnie Jean said, then took a sip of her orange soda. A few drops clung to her lips. She noticed C.J. watching her tongue as she licked off the sweet liquid.

"We were just taking a break," Nick said. "Care for a cola, Mr. Moody?"

"No." C.J. wanted to pour the remainder of the boy's cola over his head and cool him off. Why didn't a guy that young go find himself some pretty young thing? Because, C.J. thought, when a man's offered sinfully rich cheesecake, he's not about to be satisfied with plain white bread.

"I think I should introduce you two since you'll both be working here to help me get Sugar Hill ready." When Nick stood up, he offered Bonnie Jean assistance. She took his outstretched hand and pulled herself up beside him. "C.J., this is Nick Willis, Dewayne's son. I told you I planned to hire Willis and Son as the contractors to renovate this place. Nick and his men will be working here weekdays, and occasionally he'll be here on Saturdays."

"Willis." C.J. nodded in response, but made no move to shake hands with the younger man, not even when Nick offered.

Nick turned to Bonnie Jean. "Well, I think I've seen everything I needed to see here today. I'll work up those estimates and get them to you tomorrow. I'll bring them by your house."

"Thanks, Nick," Bonnie Jean said, and patted the young man on the back.

Nick grinned, then pulled her into his arms and gave her a big bear hug. "Later, pretty lady." Completely ignoring C.J., Nick opened the back screen door and stepped out into the yard.

As soon as Nick was out of sight, C.J. turned to Bonnie Jean, who was leaning against the metal lawn chair, her hip casually nudging the armrest. "A little young for you, isn't he?"

"I can't imagine what you're talking about." She reached down to the tape machine, opened it and flipped the tape over. Patsy Cline sang "Sweet Dreams." Bonnie Jean's eyes flew upward, meeting C.J.'s. She saw the cold hatred, the undisguised anger in his eyes, and wondered if he could see the fear and the pain in hers. She'd been so preoccupied with worry about being alone with C.J. that she'd forgotten this particular song was at the beginning of the tape.

How could she? he asked himself. Had she done it on purpose? Of course she had. No, no. He felt certain she didn't want to remember that night any more than he did. He never listened to country music, most especially not to Patsy Cline. Sally Vickers had kept the blasted stuff playing from morning till night. But the night he'd caught Bonnie Jean with Bubba Harland, *that* damned song had been playing. Instinctively his hand went to his belly, to the lean, scarred piece of flesh just above his groin.

Bonnie Jean's eyes followed the movement of his hand. She swallowed hard and choked back the tears that had formed in her throat. She reached down and fumbled with the cassette deck, clumsily removing the tape. It fell from her fingers and hit the floor with a loud clatter.

Just as she reached down to pick it up, C.J. stepped

in front of her. His big foot slammed down onto the tape, crushing the fragile plastic beneath his heavy weight. She gasped. He kicked the battered tape across the floor. It hit the wall and fell into several pieces, the slender thread of tape spilling across the wooden surface.

She looked up at him, and knew he was reliving that night. Damn, she hadn't meant for this to happen. Why had she been so careless? Why hadn't she remembered which song started the Patsy Cline tape? Even though she could listen to that song and not fall to pieces, obviously C.J. couldn't.

She made no attempt to pick up the tape. She stood up, ramrod straight, and faced the angry man glaring at her as if he'd like nothing better than to destroy her the way he'd destroyed the tape. When she tried to speak, the words wouldn't form on her lips.

They stood there staring at each other as memories, feelings hidden just beneath the surface, claimed them. C.J. grabbed her by the shoulders. "I could have killed you both that night." He spit the words, as if they defiled his mouth to speak them. "I actually thought that because you'd been a virgin the first time I took you that you'd never let another man touch you." His blue eyes had turned to a color so pale they seemed almost silver-white. They were filled with such rage that Bonnie Jean shivered in fear. Not really fear of C.J., but fear of what could happen.

She tried to speak, but she couldn't. She wanted to tell him the truth about that night, but what would be the use? After all this time he wouldn't believe her. Bubba's being there that night had been Sally Vickers' idea. When Bubba had arrived unexpectedly, he said he'd just dropped by to talk, and Bonnie Jean had been totally shocked when he'd crawled all over her the minute they heard C.J.'s car drive up. Within seconds Bonnie Jean's clothes were wrinkled, her hair mussed and she was trapped on the couch beneath Bubba's undulating body, her cries smothered by Bubba's mouth.

Everything had happened so quickly after that. The minute C.J. entered the living room and saw them, he'd assumed the worst. She'd never forget the look on his face or the horrible things he'd shouted at her, each word laced with contempt. Bubba had jumped to her defense, and before she knew what was happening, he and C.J. had started fighting. The fist fight quickly turned into a one-sided knife fight when Bubba pulled out his switchblade. In her nightmares, Bonnie Jean still relived the horrible moment when Bubba's knife sliced through C.J.'s shirt and left a wide gash across his lower abdomen. She'd rushed to C.J., but he'd shoved her away and staggered outside to his car. She'd followed him, crying, begging him to let her help him. With blood trickling between his fingers, he'd slipped into his Mustang and driven away.

Bonnie Jean shook her head, trying to clear away the memories of that horrible night, the last time she'd seen C.J. before he left the country, before she'd found out she was pregnant, before she'd married Bubba Harland.

She reached out and placed her hand against C.J.'s

belly, against the place, now covered by his tailored shirt, where Bubba's knife had ripped his flesh apart.

"I—I'm...sorry." The tears pooled in her eyes, but she fought to keep them from falling.

He tightened his hold on her shoulders. He didn't know if she was sorry for taking the money he later found out his mother had given her, or for sleeping with Bubba or for the knife wound in his gut. "I couldn't bear the thought of another man touching you." He jerked her up against him and threaded his fingers through her hair. "Because of you, I became an animal that night—the kind of human animal I saw all over the world—in the Middle East, in Southeast Asia. While overseas I realized that I actually had something in common with those creatures. I came home ten years ago determined to leave behind everything that wasn't pure and good and..."

"I'm sorry," she moaned, her lips moving against the front of his shirt. She'd known, of course, that he fought a never-ending battle with the fierce warrior inside himself. But she also knew that Carter Jackson Moody IV had carried his obsession with being a Southern gentleman beyond the limits of normal behavior. He was so afraid of letting go, of acting on his purely male instincts, that he'd allowed himself to become a rigid, unbending, unfeeling paragon of gentlemanly virtue. And he saw her as a threat—*the* threat—to the sterile, loveless life he'd built for himself.

"You make me hate myself," he said hoarsely. "You make me act irrationally. You always have."

"C.J., I...please don't hate yourself, and don't hate

me." She flung her arms around his waist, stood on tiptoe and kissed his chin, that hard, square chin.

She heard him groan and felt his hands move back and forth across her shoulders. He looked at her, his eyes turning bluer and bluer as they warmed with the passion coursing through him.

Her little pink tongue poked out of her mouth and flicked the cleft in his chin. He moaned and grasped her by the back of the neck. She tasted him, allowing her tongue the freedom to caress the indentation in his flesh again and again.

"Damn you, Bonnie Jean," he growled. "Damn us both."

He lowered his head and crushed her lips with his. Her mouth opened, her lips parted and she accepted the possessive thrust of his tongue. He moved his hand upward, threading his fingers through her hair, grabbing her head and holding her face against his while he ravaged her mouth. He slid his other hand down her back, slowly, tormentingly, then grabbed the rounded swell of one buttock and kneaded the flesh through her thin, faded jeans.

She clung to his shoulders, her body leaning into his, as she tilted on her toes. He was so tall, so big, so overpoweringly male. She loved the feel of him, the savage, uncontrolled part of C.J. that she alone could bring to life.

He released her mouth, but held her head, their lips almost touching. He moaned, their warm breaths mingling. "I knew coming here would be a mistake. We can't work together. We'll destroy each other." He rested his cheek against hers.

"We have a contract," she reminded him. "You're too much of a gentleman to renege on a business deal." But she knew he was right, the passion they felt was as strong as the hatred. If she insisted on following through with this business deal, would they destroy each other?

"No, I won't renege," he said so quietly she could barely hear him. "But you could release me."

"I can't."

"Don't do this to me. To yourself. I won't be taken in by you again." He released her and took one step away, trying to put some space between their heated bodies.

She felt the presence of his body so close to hers, warming her, giving her hope. She couldn't look up into his eyes. She was afraid of what she'd see. He could mask his feelings with cruel words, but the truth always showed in those expressive blue eyes of his. "Sugar Hill isn't about you and me, it's about Bonnie Jean Vickers Harland proving herself. To this town, to people like your mother, and maybe even to myself. I think I deserve this chance."

She looked so helpless, so vulnerable. But he knew it was a lie—that gentle look of innocence. How could a woman like her still look so...so pure and sweet? She was staring at him as if he were the only man she'd ever taken into her heart and into her arms and into her loving body. God, how he'd like to believe that lie. "What I want, what I deserve, is to be left in peace."

When she took a step toward him, he backed up. She wished she could give him what he said he wanted, but she had needs, too. She'd come home to Tuscumbia to find herself, to put the past to rest and move forward. But how could she when C.J. Moody stood in her way, professing he despised her? Of course, she knew it was himself he despised the most, not her. It was that primitive male animal that she aroused within him that he hated so much. "I refuse to release you from our contract."

"Damn!" He turned away from her and slammed his big fists against the wall with amazing force. The rotted wood shattered, and splinters of wood stuck in his hands. Tiny droplets of blood formed and fell freely down his hands and onto his wrists.

"Good Lord, what have you done?" Bonnie Jean cried out and ran to him, taking his injured hands into hers. Instinctively she brought his hands to her lips, kissing the bruised knuckles. "We need to see to your hands."

He pulled free of her gentle touch and glared at her, an icy wrath in his eyes. "I'm all right. I don't need your help."

"Maybe you should go," she said. "We can postpone this meeting until we're both calmer."

"Oh, no. I want to get this over with."

Bonnie Jean moved past him and into the kitchen. "I'll come to your office tomorrow. Please go. I shouldn't have asked you to come here."

He walked up behind her, but didn't touch her. He could see her shoulders moving up and down and knew she was crying. He was hurting her just as much as she was hurting him. Why was she so intent on putting them both through this when she had to know they could never be business partners?

"Call me when you have those estimates from Willis," he said.

She didn't respond verbally. She nodded her head and walked out into the hallway and toward the front door. He watched as she turned and dashed up the stairs. First he heard a door slam shut, then a wild, wounded scream, and finally utter silence. The pain that ripped through him at that moment was as fierce and excruciating as the one he'd experienced when Bubba Harland had ripped open his gut. But this time the pain wasn't physical, and he didn't know if it would ever heal.

C.J. Moody walked outside into the bright September sunshine, got into his Mercedes and drove away.

Four

The next few weeks were an exercise in torture for Bonnie Jean, and she suspected they were for C.J., too. But neither one would give more than an inch. When either of them seemed to make a step forward, natural wariness of the other would soon have them taking two steps backward.

During the month that Wheeler had vacationed in Saint Croix with Mrs. Jeffreys, Bonnie Jean and C.J. had set things in motion and work was well under way at the old Moody house. Everything was moving so quickly and smoothly that Bonnie Jean anticipated a New Year's Eve opening for the restaurant.

She and C.J. had been together more often than either of them had wanted to be. Never once did he lose his temper again or remind her of their past love affair. He had made sure a third party was always present, and he discussed nothing but business.

Wheeler had been disappointed when she'd told him that he should forget any silly notion he had of getting her and C.J. together again. After all, when a man was determined to never forgive a woman and she was unable to forget the pain he'd caused her, there was little hope of a reconciliation.

The smell of dirt and hay and manure mixed with the aroma of human sweat, animal scents and tobacco smoke. But the unusual mixture didn't bother Bonnie Jean or her companions. They were old rodeo fans, and the action inside the ring more than compensated for the odors.

A deep Southern voice announced the next event, the sound reverberating from the loudspeaker system. Excitement filled the grandstands where hordes of cheering spectators watched while one man and one steer battled for supremacy.

"Here's your orange soda," Nick said, handing Bonnie Jean her drink as he sat down between her and Elaine. "Looks like it's blowing up a rain out there. We'll be lucky to get out of here before the bottom falls out."

"Oh, hush your complaining. A little rain won't make you melt," Elaine teased. "Besides, you'll look scrumptious with your wet shirt plastered to your chest."

"You two are indecent." Bonnie Jean took a swig from the orange drink can. "I guess you know you're corrupting my morals."

Wheeler Yancey removed his brown Stetson and wiped the perspiration from his forehead with the back of his hand. "Would you take a look at that?"

Three sets of eyes focused on the ring where a burly young cowboy was wrestling a steer to the earth and adeptly roping it.

"He's good," Elaine said. "And kind of cute, too."

"Hey, watch that," Nick said. "You're not supposed to notice how cute other guys are."

"I don't see anything so spectacular about him or his roping," Bonnie Jean said, turning to Wheeler.

"I wasn't talking about Hinton's looks or his skill. What caught my attention wasn't in the ring, but up here in the grandstands. Over there." He nodded down and to their left.

Bonnie Jean saw him immediately. He looked gorgeous. Perfectly attired, perfectly groomed. C.J. Moody wore stone-washed black jeans, a gray cotton shirt, and a black Stetson. He sat and crossed his legs, revealing the gleaming black snakeskin boots on his feet. The leather belt strapped around his waist sported a huge metal buckle.

"I didn't think he'd be able to stay away," Bonnie Jean said.

"Nope. Once the rodeo gets in your blood, part of it's there to stay. That boy was good, wasn't he? Damned good." Wheeler turned to Bonnie Jean.

"Why are you looking at me like that?" she asked.

"If he'd married you instead of Kathie Lou, he never would have given up his favorite hobby. My bet is, he'd still be riding broncos every now and then just for the hell of it.''

She felt a hard lump form in her throat, and a frisson of pain shot through her heart. ''But he didn't marry me. He married the *lady* his mama picked out for him.''

''I wonder if Thea picked out that lady he's with today?''

Bonnie Jean hadn't even noticed the female sitting beside C.J. until Wheeler pointed her out. ''It's Barbara Massey!''

''So it is. Now what do you suppose he's doing with her?'' Wheeler chuckled. ''Looks like her brother's with them.''

''Oliver Merritt,'' Bonnie Jean said, taking quick and hopefully discreet glances in their direction. ''A couple of winners there. Two of the biggest Southern snobs that ever walked the face of the earth.''

''A couple of idiots who just happened to inherit land and money,'' Wheeler said.

''Dorothea would probably be thrilled to see C.J. paired off with Barbara. Her blood's almost as blue as his.''

''C.J.'s not going to let anybody pick out a wife for him again, and I don't think his taste in women runs to tall, skinny redheads with two ex-husbands.''

Bonnie Jean clasped the aluminum drink can in her hand so tightly that the sides dented and orange soda sloshed out the top, spilling onto her hands. ''Damn!'' She set the drink can on the bleachers beside her and wiped off the sticky sweet liquid with a handkerchief she'd pulled from her jeans pocket.

"Don't get your feathers ruffled, gal. I doubt C.J. brought Barbara here. More than likely she and Oliver came together and she's just latched herself onto C.J."

"Maybe you're right. She's hardly his type, but she's had a thing for C.J. since we were in high school."

"Hey, you want me to run outside and put the top up on your Caddy?" Nick asked.

"What?" Bonnie Jean said, only halfway listening to her future brother-in-law.

"You left the top down on your car," Nick said. "It's starting to rain."

"Oh. No, thanks, Nick, I'll go. I need some fresh air anyway." Bonnie Jean patted Wheeler on the back when she got up. "I think I'm going to go on. You mind catching a ride with Elaine and Nick?"

"It's not like you to run away, gal. You're not giving up the fight, are you?"

"I need to be working instead of taking a day off for the rodeo," she said, then leaned over and kissed Wheeler on the cheek.

C.J. tried to smile at Barbara, but he simply wasn't able to listen to her girlish chatter. She'd cornered him when he'd first arrived, latched herself onto his arm, and wouldn't take a polite no for an answer. She was pretty enough, he supposed, if your taste ran to long and lean, but she was a chatty, frivolous woman with a great deal of empty space between her ears. He had dated her a couple of times when she'd still been in high school, and he'd found out then that she was a catty little snob who went out with him because he was Carter Jackson Moody IV and not because she liked him personally.

"I absolutely despise rodeos," Barbara said, running her fingertips over her stylishly short hair. "But Oliver insisted I join him today. He and Frances are on the outs again. I've told him to divorce her, but he keeps going back for more misery."

"I wish you wouldn't discuss my personal life so freely." Oliver Merritt glared at his sister.

"Oh, hush, Ollie, and watch your stupid rodeo." Barbara slipped her arm through C.J.'s. Her hand rested against his thigh, and she squeezed his leg tightly. "I'm looking forward to the charity auction next month. You are going, aren't you?"

"Uh-huh." He saw Bonnie Jean get up, bend over and kiss Wheeler, and he felt that sickening coil of jealousy rip at his insides. Where the hell is she going? he wondered.

"I just adore going to the country club. I haven't seen you there lately."

"Excuse me," C.J. said as he stood up. "I've got something I must do right now."

She looked up at him with big, questioning eyes, then laughed with understanding. "Oh. Of course. I'll just sit here with Oliver until you get back. I'd love to discuss the auction with you. I'm going to do my best to persuade you to be my date."

C.J. made his way down the bleachers and through the crowd. When he stepped outside, soft pellets of cool rain hit him. He saw several people rushing toward their vehicles and realized they were hurrying to put up the tops on their cars and Jeeps.

He caught a glimpse of Bonnie Jean scurrying toward her old red Cadillac. What the hell was the matter with him? Why had he followed her? Exactly where had he thought she was going? She'd left both Wheeler and that young stud, Willis, sitting back in the grandstands. Had he thought she was rushing out to meet a third man? He had to admit the thought had crossed his mind. Why did he always think the worst of Bonnie Jean? It was obvious that men found her attractive. Hell, he found her attractive. But he had to admit that, except for the gossip about her and Wheeler, there had been no talk about her involvement with a man since Bubba's death.

Lately he seemed to be at war with himself. Old feelings, long buried, had begun to resurface, but he was afraid of those emotions, those primitive needs over which he had little control when he was around Bonnie Jean.

He watched as she struggled with the cloth top of her convertible. Probably stuck, he thought. Old cars had a way of acting up at the most inappropriate times.

The rain poured down, becoming heavier and cooler as the autumn sky exploded with lightning. She was getting soaked to the skin. It was obvious she needed help. Without thinking, C.J. dashed out into the downpour and made his way quickly to Bonnie Jean's car. Not saying a word, he helped her complete the task. She stood there on the driver's side of the car staring at him. He stared back. Rain drenched them both.

When a sharp crack of lightning rent the sky apart, C.J. hollered above the boom of thunder that followed. "Let's get in the car."

Simultaneously they opened the doors and jumped inside. Quickly they rolled up the windows on their respective sides of the Caddy, then fell backward, resting their wet heads on cushioned seats. C.J. reached up, removed his Stetson and tossed it into the back seat.

Bonnie Jean took in several deep breaths. Suddenly her body trembled from the chilly dampness of her wet clothes. She wanted to look at him, to ask him what he was doing outside, but she didn't. She ran nervous fingers through her soaked hair. "Thanks."

"You should have sent Willis out here to put up the top," C.J. said.

She closed her eyes and counted to ten. She'd forgotten how jealous C.J. had acted over Nick the first time they'd met at the old Moody house. She should have told C.J. then that Nick was Elaine's fiancé, but she had wanted him to trust her. *But why should you expect him to trust you now? He didn't trust you years ago when he loved you.*

"Or he could have come with you, then y'all could have made out in the car. It's warm and dry in here. And with all this rain nobody could see in." C.J. ran his index finger across the windshield, creating a clean line along the misty window. "Besides, in a few minutes the windows will be completely fogged."

Bonnie Jean turned around and looked at him. She

pulled one leg up on the seat, bending her knee so that it almost touched him. She ran her hand through her hair again, then shook her head. She unbuttoned the top two buttons of her gold-studded chambray shirt and ran her hand across her collarbone and down inside, rubbing the moisture into her skin. She looked at him and smiled.

"I didn't want to bother Nick or Wheeler since I was leaving to go home," she said. "What were you doing? Surely you weren't deserting your date."

C.J. wished she'd stop rubbing the rain into her skin. With her shirt partially unbuttoned, he had a perfect view of exposed flesh—warm, tanned flesh. He could see the inside curve of her breasts where the shirt hung open, and the hardened tips pouted through the wet material. "What date?"

"The skinny redhead." Bonnie Jean started massaging her neck with one hand and rubbing her thigh with the other.

"Are you talking about Barbara?"

"Is that her name?"

"You know damned well what her name is. You went to school with her for years."

"You were sitting with her, weren't you?"

"She was sitting with me." C.J. wondered if Bonnie Jean was actually jealous. He hoped so. He wanted her to know the agony he went through thinking of her with other men. "Barbara's an old friend."

"Oh. I see. Your mother approves of her, I'm sure."

"Barbara and Mother belong to some of the same clubs."

"Other than the fact that she, too, has a pedigree, I can't imagine what the two of you have in common. I remember in seventh grade when she assured Mrs. Richmond that her father most certainly knew all about the law of gravity since he was a lawyer."

C.J. couldn't suppress a chuckle. Barbara's air-headed behavior was legendary in Tuscumbia, as were her numerous affairs. "I can assure you that Oliver is her intellectual equal."

"Oliver is a pain in the behind," Bonnie Jean said.

"He seems to like your company. I understand he eats at The Plantation almost every weekday."

"He likes to flirt. And not just with me, but with all my waitresses. He seems to think women in our profession are fair game. His reasoning is that if we were ladies we wouldn't have to work as waitresses."

"How does Willis feel about your profession?" C.J. asked.

"Dewayne Willis and his son Nick are delighted that I'm a restaurateur. After all, I've hired them as my contractors for Sugar Hill."

"Why can't you date a man closer to your age? Willis can't be a day over thirty, and Uncle Wheeler's sixty-five."

Bonnie Jean moved her bent knee, slowly edging her body across the seat. "I don't happen to be dating either man. Nick is Elaine's fiancé, and Wheeler is my good friend."

"Nick Willis is engaged to Elaine?" Damn Bonnie Jean for making him feel like a fool. No. No. He'd done that all by himself by assuming the worst. He had allowed his mistrust of her to make him act stupidly. "You like playing games, don't you? You enjoy seeing me lose control!"

"I should have explained who Nick was when you first met. I owe you an apology."

"Maybe I owe you one, too. After all, I jumped to all the wrong conclusions. I automatically thought the worst of you."

"I know."

"So, if Nick is engaged and Uncle Wheeler is just a good friend, who's the man in your life now?" He couldn't imagine a woman as beautiful and sensual as Bonnie Jean going long without a man.

"There isn't anyone. I'm not interested in a relationship right now."

"What about Eddie McWilliams?" He knew she'd dated Eddie a few times after she'd come back to Tuscumbia, but old Eddie had remarried and divorced since then.

It was all Bonnie Jean could do to control her laughter. "Eddie?" Good grief, she hadn't thought of Eddie in at least two years. Once she'd realized the only thing Eddie wanted was a roll in the hay, she'd said adios. Oh, Eddie was fun to be with, and not bad-looking either, but she had no desire to have him as a lover.

"Well, what about Eddie?"

She edged closer and closer until her knee rested on his leg. She slipped her arms around his neck. "I haven't seen Eddie since his last divorce. What does this make, number four?"

Suddenly C.J. realized she was practically sitting

in his lap and had herself wrapped around him like a snake around a branch. ''Bonnie Jean—''

''I'm glad you reminded me that Eddie is a free man again. Maybe I'll give him a call and—''

He cut off her words with his mouth. He hadn't intended to kiss her. It had been the last thing on his mind, but somehow it seemed the only thing to do, the one and only thing he wanted to do.

She melted into him, her mouth opening, her body softening. He clutched her by the hips and completed the task of placing her body in his lap.

He hadn't meant for this to happen. He never did. But, somehow, just being around Bonnie Jean made him act irrationally. God, her mouth was sweet! Her lips were soft, her breath hot.

He deepened the kiss. She responded, her tongue moving to the same primitive rhythm as his. Bonnie Jean threaded her fingers through his thick silver hair while her other hand burrowed between their bodies. He groaned when he felt her fingers slip between the snaps of his shirt, her nails scratching at his chest hair.

She unsnapped his shirt with one quick jerk on the front. He released her mouth and stared into her sparkling eyes, eyes so bright, so warm they mesmerized him.

''You make me crazy,'' he admitted, then reached down to unbutton her shirt.

She watched while he moved his big, dark hands, slowly releasing one button at a time and gliding his fingers over each new inch of exposed flesh. When he reached her belt, he stopped and spread the soft material away from her body.

"You're too old to be running around without a bra," he said, staring at her naked breasts, his hands clutching the sides of her shirt.

"Do I need a bra?" she asked, her heart wild, her mind floating.

He took both breasts in his hands, tenderly squeezing their firm fullness. "No."

She didn't know if she could bear much more of this ecstasy. It had been so long since he'd touched her like this. "I want to feel you against me." She spread his shirt and moved her breasts across his hairy chest. Her nipples hardened with desire.

He grabbed her by the shoulders and moved her body back and forth against his, gently at first and then roughly. With an unleased passion, he lowered his head and took one protruding nipple into his mouth. His lips encompassed, his teeth nipped, his tongue tortured. Bonnie Jean felt him hardening, and squirmed her bottom against his arousal.

"Damn, I want you." C.J. switched his attention to her other breast.

"I want you, too," she moaned when his lips closed over her flesh and began sucking.

C.J. released her breast and ran his tongue upward toward her collarbone. "How the hell can you sleep with any other man?" he demanded, the surging jealousy building inside him. The very thought that another man had known the pleasures of her beautiful body angered him. If he had his way, no other man would ever touch her.

"What makes you think I do?"

He pulled away and stared at her, not sure he'd heard her correctly. "What are you saying?"

"There isn't anyone else."

"Are you saying you haven't slept with anyone since Bubba died?" His body was coiled as tight as a spring. He was hard and hungry and wanted Bonnie Jean to the point of madness, but he refused to take her. She wasn't the kind of woman who'd be faithful. All those years ago when he'd loved her so desperately, when he'd been so certain he was the only man in her life, she'd been giving herself to Bubba Harland.

"Would you believe me if I said that I'm nothing like my mother, that I never have been? There hasn't been a parade of men in and out of my life. I have to be committed to a man before I give myself to him." She was telling him the truth, but she could see the doubt in his pale blue eyes.

"I'd like to believe that." More than he needed air to breathe, he needed to believe her. But he couldn't. He was afraid.

"Then do."

"I can't." He pulled the sides of her shirt together, covering her tempting breasts. "I've known you too long."

"You're judging me on the basis of a family I didn't ask to be born into."

"I know who and what you came from, Bonnie Jean." He began snapping his shirt. "There was a time when I thought you were different."

"You still believe I betrayed you, and you'll never forgive me for that night."

"You're like a wild animal, honey. A savage little beast who brings out the beast in me. I could have killed you and Bubba that night, and I swore I'd never let you have that much control over me again." He reached in the back seat and picked up his Stetson.

Her cheeks flared crimson, and heat suffused her whole body. How dare he accuse her of bringing out the worst in him! His sainted mother and that fragile wife of his had been the ones who'd turned him into a stiff-necked, snobbish *gentleman*. As far as Bonnie Jean was concerned, they had turned a real man into a weak imitation. "I like the beast in you. He's far more human than Carter Jackson Moody IV."

C.J. put the Stetson on his head and opened the car door. A gush of cool air and rain hit him the moment he stepped outside. Bonnie Jean scooted across the seat to the open door.

"Stay away from me, Bonnie Jean. What I feel for you is lust, and I'm strong enough to resist my baser urges."

"Fine with me," she said. "Why should I care if you walk around with a hard-on? I don't need you in my life. All you ever gave me was misery."

He stopped dead still for a split second, then began walking faster and faster as the rain drenched him to the skin. Suddenly he broke into a run, his long legs taking him as far away from Bonnie Jean Harland as he could go. All he could think about were the words with which she'd taunted him, "Would you believe me if I told you I'm nothing like my mother, that I never have been? There hasn't been a parade of men in and out of my life." Dear God, he wanted to believe it was the truth, but he knew it couldn't be. Could it?

Bonnie Jean pulled the car door closed. With trembling fingers, she rebuttoned her wet shirt. *I will not cry. I will not cry.* She hugged herself, rocking back and forth in the front seat of her old red Caddy. Silent tears fell from her eyes.

Five

―――――

"I can't believe he brought that woman here!" Barbara Massey said, her big brown eyes gleaming with resentment as she watched Wheeler Yancey and Bonnie Jean Harland enter the country club.

C.J. acknowledged his date's statement with a grunt, but he didn't take his eyes off Bonnie Jean Harland until she and his uncle disappeared inside the antebellum mansion. He'd been watching her discreetly ever since she'd arrived at the Addie Fenner Study Club Charity Auction.

"It's disgraceful the way your uncle flaunts his relationship with that strumpet." Barbara blotted the moisture from her cheeks with a lace handkerchief, and turned to C.J.'s mother and Dorothea's friend Polly Drew.

"I doubt he gives you or any other woman a

thought when he's with Bonnie Jean," Polly said, smiling. She touched C.J. on the arm. "Isn't that right, Carter?"

"What?" He wasn't listening to Polly. His mind was on the woman who had absolutely no business being here today. Her presence would ruin the pleasant Saturday afternoon he'd planned to share with his mother and Barbara.

"If you were spending the day with Bonnie Jean, would you be thinking of any other woman?" Polly asked.

"What an absurd question," Barbara said. "Carter would never waste his time with a woman like that."

"Just what sort of woman do you think Ms. Harland is?" Dorothea Moody asked, the words spoken in a tight, clipped voice.

"Well, Dorothea, her family did live on Sugar Hill. The whole town knows what sort her mother was. And it's no secret Bonnie Jean got herself pregnant by that awful Bubba Harland before they ran off to Nashville." Barbara smiled ever so sweetly.

"That's all history," Dorothea said. "It seems since she returned to Tuscumbia four years ago, she's lived an exemplary life. And she's quite successful as a businesswoman. Wheeler tells me she sold her Nashville restaurant for a handsome profit."

"Shall we go inside, ladies?" C.J. asked, deliberately avoiding any comment on his mother's surprising defense of Bonnie Jean Harland. "It's almost two, and the auction should be starting soon."

"Very well," Barbara said, and took her escort's right arm while Dorothea accepted the left. "And don't forget that I expect you to bid on that Crane mantel clock. I have my heart set on it. Wouldn't it make a nice birthday present for me?''

''I promise to bid on it, but I've already set my limit for it and for the block-front chest I want,'' C.J. said.

During the past month since his encounter with Bonnie Jean in the rodeo parking lot, he'd been dating Barbara Massey. Why, he wasn't sure for the life of him, except he knew how much Bonnie Jean detested the woman. They'd been enemies since grammar school. The brainy blond bombshell from the wrong side of the tracks and the air-headed redhead who'd been born into Colbert county's social elite. It was getting more and more difficult to stay away from Bonnie Jean, more difficult to stop thinking about her and wanting to be with her. He supposed if he could use dating Barbara as a barrier between Bonnie Jean and him, then it was worth listening to the boring Ms. Massey's inane chatter on their dates.

C.J. led Barbara and his mother inside the country club. Polly Drew followed close behind, stopping occasionally to speak to friends and acquaintances.

''There's some seats right over there,'' Polly said, pointing to vacant chairs directly across the aisle from Wheeler and Bonnie Jean.

C.J. seated the ladies, then himself, and turned slightly in order to glance around the room. The doors connecting the front and back parlors had been opened and filled with folding chairs. A podium was set up against one wall, and the auctioneer stood on it, scanning the audience.

Casually, as if by accident, C.J.'s gaze stopped on Bonnie Jean. She looked gorgeous today, every inch the lady. His thoughts went back eighteen years to a time when she'd wanted so badly to be "good enough for him." She had worried constantly that she wasn't a real lady like his mother and that she'd never fit into his life. Now he wondered if that display of insecurity had been an act, if she'd ever given a damn about pleasing him, about being accepted by his family.

How could she still be so beautiful, after all this time? She wasn't a young girl anymore. She was thirty-six. But the years had only matured her figure into womanly curves and given her an air of self-assurance that made her undeniably attractive to any red-blooded man.

Although his view was restricted by the crowd, he didn't have to see her completely to know precisely what she wore and how she looked. He hadn't been able to keep his eyes off her when they'd been outside. He'd been irritated by the hungry looks other men gave her. He had wanted to shout, *Look, but don't touch, because she belongs to me.* But she didn't belong to him. He wasn't sure she ever had.

He glanced in her direction again, enjoying the sight of her with her hair hanging loosely about her shoulders, the platinum curls streaked with pale gold. Elegant pearl-and-diamond earrings matched the strand of pearls around her neck, and the hunter-green suit she wore accented her tiny waist, full breasts and gently rounded hips. She was a woman any man would be proud to introduce to his friends, proud to be seen with.

He watched her smiling at Wheeler, talking and laughing as she laced her arm through the old man's and squeezed tightly. C.J. felt his insides constrict and a gut-level pain spread through him. Every time he saw the two of them together, it both angered and hurt him. Even though he was reasonably sure Bonnie Jean wasn't having an affair with his uncle, he couldn't quite figure out their relationship. Ever since she'd moved back to Tuscumbia four years ago, Wheeler Yancey had been the woman's champion. But what puzzled C.J. even more was his mother's recent change in attitude. Eighteen years ago, his mother had made no secret of the fact that she adamantly opposed C.J.'s relationship with Sally Vickers's daughter. When he'd told his mother that he'd asked Bonnie Jean to marry him, Dorothea Moody had ranted and raved like a madwoman. But, for the past few months, C.J. had heard his mother defending Bonnie Jean on more than one occasion.

Quiet filled the Fenner Country Club when the auction began. C.J. forced himself to concentrate on the first item up for bid, a tin bird roaster, but as soon as the bidding started, he glanced back in Bonnie Jean's direction and caught her staring at him. She smiled, put her hand up to her cheek and waved with the tips of her fingers.

C.J.'s eyes widened. He looked away from her immediately, and surveyed the crowd to see if anyone had noticed Bonnie Jean's flirty wave. A warm flush seeped into his face as he turned toward Barbara.

"You should speak to your uncle," Barbara said. "It's one thing if he wants to continue his back-street affair with that woman, but it's disgraceful for him to bring her to social functions. Really, it looks bad for your whole family."

C.J. nodded, but didn't reply.

"To think that he actually brought her here. Dorothea, you must be terribly embarrassed."

C.J. had endured a similar conversation with his mother numerous times in the past, and he could understand now if she were upset at seeing Bonnie Jean here. He well knew her feelings concerning her precious study club, named in honor of her grandmother, and held at the country club named in honor of her great-grandfather, one of the early citizens of the county. But, it rankled him to have to listen to Barbara Massey's constant put-downs. Bonnie Jean had never had Barbara's advantages, but she'd matured into a beautiful lady, far more desirable as a mate than Barbara would ever be.

Polly Drew nudged Dorothea on the arm. "Why don't you tell Barbara how you feel about Bonnie Jean being here with Wheeler today?"

Dorothea turned to her son and placed her small, delicate hand on his arm. "I think it's high time people gave that poor girl a chance."

"People are never going to forget where she came from and who her mother was," Barbara said.

"Wheeler thinks quite highly of her," Dorothea said, still speaking to C.J. "And he isn't having an affair with Bonnie Jean. They're friends and business associates."

"Teenie Jeffreys is Wheeler's girlfriend," Polly Drew said. "She's been his sweetie for the past six months. Honestly, Barbara, you've been misinformed about Bonnie Jean Harland."

"Well," Barbara huffed. "Polly Drew, I can't understand why you'd defend her, even if your niece did lower herself enough to befriend that creature."

Dorothea turned her attention to the next item up for bid. "Oh, Carter, those glass spice keepers would make a lovely Christmas present for your cousin Maud," she said, and made a bid.

Relieved that his mother had ended the discussion, C.J. couldn't resist taking a peek at Bonnie Jean. He cut his eyes to the right, careful not to move even a fraction and draw attention to himself. She was still looking at him, damn her, and smiling like a spoiled child who'd just gotten away with something naughty.

Bonnie Jean knew she had embarrassed C.J., and was delighted. Serves him right, she thought, and was tempted to wave at him again. But he looked away before she had a second chance. She'd hated the thought of coming to this snobby auction, but when Wheeler reminded her it would be an excellent opportunity to pick up some of the antiques to furnish Sugar Hill, she agreed to attend.

Barbara Massey had been giving her the evil eye since they'd arrived. But she'd come too far, and accomplished too much in her thirty-six years, to let the likes of Barbara Merritt Massey hurt her. She didn't give a tinker's damn what that rich, spoiled woman thought of her. But she did care very much what Dorothea Moody thought of her, and only hoped that

Barbara's poisoned tongue hadn't influenced Dorothea's benevolent new attitude.

"Fifty dollars," Wheeler said, raising the bid on a cat-shaped boot scraper.

Bonnie Jean laughed when no one outbid her companion. She wondered what on earth he was going to do with the unusual metal object he'd just acquired. "Going to scrape your boots with it?"

Wheeler grunted, but smiled good-naturedly. "Item number ten, gal. Listen. It's that chest you want."

She turned her attention to the auctioneer, whose glowing description of the lovely old piece made Bonnie Jean want it all the more.

"This is an exceptional piece of furniture, ladies and gentlemen. A handsome block-front chest. A John Townsend original. Late 1700s. Please note that the chest has alternating concave and convex hand-carved shells with delicate fluting and cross-hatching in the centers."

Bonnie Jean could picture the chest in the foyer of Sugar Hill. She wondered what it would go for. When she heard the auctioneer quote a starting bid, she made several mental calculations and decided on the absolute top price she'd pay.

After two bids were made, Bonnie Jean said, "Three hundred dollars."

"Thank you, ma'am. Three hundred…three hundred, who'll make it three-fifty?" the auctioneer asked.

"Three-fifty," C.J. Moody said.

Bonnie Jean jerked her head around and stared at

him. Was he doing this to aggravate her, or did he really want the chest? "Three-seventy-five."

Another bid was made by someone Bonnie Jean didn't know, then the contest became an exclusive duel between C.J. and her. The price rose steadily, until she neared her limit. She was tempted to keep bidding, regardless of the cost, but refused to give in to the desire to outdo C.J.

Bonnie Jean made her final bid. Several moments passed before she looked at a silent C.J. Very slowly, he turned to her, his eyes cold but triumphant, as if he knew she'd gone her limit. He outbid her fifty dollars while looking her squarely in the eye.

When she made no further bid, Wheeler leaned over and whispered in her ear. "Go higher if you want, gal. I'll pay the extra."

So like Wheeler, she thought. Generous to a fault. "No, let him have it. He's determined to see I don't acquire that piece, and he'll probably pay three times what it's worth if necessary."

Item after item went to the highest bidder. Dorothea Moody made another purchase as did her friend Polly. When Wheeler acquired a pine cradle, he received numerous odd stares. Bonnie Jean smothered a giggle when he winked at her as if saying, "Let 'em think what they want about that one." The auction continued, and Bonnie Jean tried to forget that C.J. sat across the aisle. However, when he outbid her on two other items, she realized that he was not a man she could ignore.

Polly Drew had just purchased a mahogany tea

caddy when Barbara Massey tapped C.J. on the arm. "The clock's up for bid next, Carter."

He nodded, and listened while the auctioneer recited the item's noteworthy qualities. "A Crane mantel clock, housed in solid cherry. This clock has a special feature. It requires winding only once a year."

"I've got to have it," Bonnie Jean told Wheeler. "That clock is going on the mantel in the foyer."

The bidding started, and Bonnie Jean jumped in sooner than she'd intended, her desire for the item overruling caution. C.J. entered the contest, and she felt her heart sink. Damn his contrary hide, she thought. Well, buddy, this one's mine, no matter what I have to pay for it.

The bidding narrowed down to Bonnie Jean and C.J., the price slightly above the true value of the clock. C.J. glanced at her, and she smiled back at him.

"Don't let that woman outbid you, Carter," Barbara said. "I don't care what you have to pay for that clock. Just keep bidding."

And so the bidding continued until the price escalated to double the item's value. The crowd buzzed with excitement, and several community grandams began to whisper, while their husbands watched Bonnie Jean stand to make her next bid. C.J. felt an undeniable rage build inside him when he noticed all the men gaping at her, undressing her with their eyes.

C.J. raised the bid by a hundred dollars, and a hushed quiet fell over the country club.

Bonnie Jean shifted her feet, inadvertently thrusting one well-rounded hip toward C.J. She toyed with the pearl ring on her finger, and glared across the aisle.

The entire crowd watched the two adversaries, everyone's attention moving back and forth from one side of the room to the other.

Bonnie Jean raised the bid by another hundred. Several loud gasps, numerous murmurs, and a few discreet laughs caught C.J.'s attention. She was making a fool of him, he thought. He no longer gave a damn that Barbara had wanted the clock. He'd kept bidding because he'd wanted to outdo Bonnie Jean Harland. But his actions had only brought attention to himself and the woman he was trying to best. This auction, or rather his part in it, would be a hot gossip item for weeks to come. Hell, it was like old times, the two of them doing something totally ridiculous and loving every minute of it. Eighteen years ago, they'd had this whole town buzzing for months. A couple of wild, carefree kids, in love with each other and with life.

C.J. groaned and ran the back of his hand over his face. Old times be damned. He wasn't that young hellion who didn't care what people thought about him, and Bonnie Jean wasn't the innocent girl for whom he'd broken all the rules.

Let her have the clock! All he wanted was to put an end to this sordid display of emotions.

C.J. remained silent, and the auctioneer asked again for a higher bid. Barbara grabbed C.J.'s arm. "I want that clock."

He closed his eyes, wanting to tell her to go straight to hell. But of course he wouldn't. He was, after all, a Southern gentleman, and respect for a lady ranked high among his priorities.

C.J. raised the bid by fifty. The crowd turned their attention across the aisle.

Bonnie Jean felt like one of the prized antiques on display. Every person in the two parlors was looking right at her. Still standing, she turned and looked down at Wheeler.

"Do it right, gal," he said. "Show 'em your stuff."

Bonnie Jean took a deep breath, blinked her eyes once and raised the bid five hundred dollars. The crowd went wild. Several older ladies swooned, more than one woman denounced Bonnie Jean, and Dorothea Moody delicately wiped the perspiration from her face. Polly Drew covered her mouth and laughed until tears streamed down her cheeks.

C.J. stiffened, his jaw clenched tightly, and his hands balled into fists. He placed his hands on top of his thighs, and damned himself for allowing this to happen. God, what he'd give to be able to get his hands on that woman. He could see the headlines now: Newspaper Editor Kills Gorgeous Blond Restaurateur.

"Carter!" Barbara didn't try to disguise her fury.

"For heaven's sake, leave him alone," Polly said, barely able to control her laughter. "Can't you see he's mortified? You don't want to give him a heart attack."

Barbara dug her fingers into C.J.'s sleeve. "Make another bid."

"No." Dorothea Moody said.

Barbara stared at C.J.'s mother, astonishment and anger contorting her aristocratic face. "Then I will."

"No, Barbara, you won't," C.J. said.

The room stilled, as if everyone had taken a deep breath and was holding it. The auctioneer awarded the prize to Ms. Harland, and the crowd released its breath. C.J. stood and walked down the aisle. Barbara sat stiffly in her seat, not even acknowledging his departure.

Wheeler nudged Bonnie Jean and said, "Now might be a good time to get some fresh air."

She nodded agreement, and the two followed C.J. outside to the immaculately groomed country club grounds. Bonnie Jean watched him walk toward his Mercedes, and wondered if he intended to leave his mother and Barbara without transportation home. Had their little fiasco inside angered him so that he could actually forget his precious good manners?

C.J. leaned against the front fender of the car and rubbed his forehead, then pulled a red silk handkerchief from the pocket of his gray-and-white-plaid sports coat and wiped the perspiration from his hands. He wanted to drive off and keep driving until he was a thousand miles away from Bonnie Jean Harland. Every time she got near him, he made a fool of himself.

He gazed back at the country club and saw Wheeler and Bonnie Jean standing a few feet from the front veranda. They smiled and talked and laughed. Laughing at him, no doubt.

Then she turned her brilliant smile on him and started walking in his direction. Surely she didn't intend to gloat about the spectacle they'd made of themselves? But, knowing her penchant for stirring up trouble, maybe she did.

C.J. couldn't stop himself from smiling. Bonnie Jean had been driving him crazy for the past few months, but he had to admit that it had been years since he'd felt so alive. All those years ago, she'd brought something into his life that had always been missing, and no other woman had ever filled the void. A great deal of it was the sex, but there had been a lot more to their relationship. There had been the love—so deep, so complete that even after eighteen years, it was still a part of him. And there had been the fun, the joy, the pleasure in simply being alive and together. He'd never known that until Bonnie Jean came into his life, and he'd never known it again until…until lately.

The realization struck him like a lightning bolt. Even though he didn't trust Bonnie Jean and was afraid to risk loving her again, he had enjoyed their confrontations, their mental sparring matches, their physical encounters. She was bringing him back to life again, and it felt good. Damn good!

She stopped directly in front of him, only a few inches separating their bodies as they stood between C.J.'s white Mercedes and a Lincoln Continental. He looked down at her feet. She wore green suede, open-toed pumps, and every stocking-covered toenail sparkled with pale peach polish.

"I didn't mean for things to get out of hand like that," she said.

His gaze moved up her long, shapely legs, over the green woolen material of her skirt and stopped at the rounded thrust of her breasts beneath her fitted jacket. "Yes, you did."

"Why must you always assume the worst about me?"

He felt his whole body react. He balled his hands into fists and raised his eyes to her face. "You won today's little skirmish, honey, but the war's far from over."

"We don't have to fight. Things don't have to be this way between us."

"Are you suggesting a truce?" Blood surged through his big body with an invigorating force. He wanted to grab her by the shoulders and demand that she tell him that she'd never loved Bubba Harland, that she'd never betrayed him with the other man.

"I'm asking for an end to the war we've been fighting for the past—" She caught herself before she said the past eighteen years. "For the past couple of years, since Laurel...." She saw him flinch. So his pride's still hurting, she thought. "Anyway, since we've been coming into contact so often, we always wind up making a spectacle of ourselves."

"Are you saying that it's my fault?" He knew it was as much his fault as hers. Was it possible that what happened eighteen years ago could have, in some way, been partly his fault, too?

"Yes, it is. If you didn't freeze me out, treat me as if I'm some sort of subhuman species, then I wouldn't react the way I do."

"Ahh. So you are admitting you deliberately try to get a rise out of me." The moment he said the words, he wished them back.

Bonnie Jean grinned, trying hard not to laugh. Her smile widened, and she burst into laughter.

"Dammit, you know what I meant!"

"Oh, but…you were right." She couldn't stop laughing. "I do try to rile you."

"And you enjoy doing it."

"Look, C.J., why don't we just admit the truth? As much as we'd both like to deny it, we're still interested in each other." She hadn't wanted to still care, to still long for a man who'd not only mistrusted her, but had made her pay dearly for a sin she'd never committed.

"The only interest I have in you, honey, is seeing that your blasted restaurant makes big profits for Yancey-Moody Enterprises," he lied to her, but he could no longer lie to himself. His interest in her had very little to do with their business deal and everything to do with the two of them as lovers.

"Don't do this, C.J." She leaned toward him, her breasts grazing the front of his chest.

He felt the sweat trickling down his spine and could hear the roar of his own rapid heartbeat drumming in his ears. She was a witch, with her husky voice, pale blond hair, and ripe body. He wanted to touch her, but he didn't. When he looked into her eyes, he felt himself drowning in their hungry gaze, so he glanced over her shoulder and forced himself to concentrate on the rows of parked cars. Dear God, he wanted her, but if he ever took her, there would be no turning back. He'd never be able to give her up.

"If you were fighting me, you might have a chance

of winning." She reached out and ran the back of her knuckles across his cheek.

He pulled away from her hand and tried to turn. She moved her body closer to his, trapping him against his car.

"You're not fighting me," she said. "You're fighting yourself, and it's a losing battle. Sooner or later that iron will of yours is going to break, and you could destroy us both."

"If you're afraid, then why don't you stay the hell away from me?" He pushed his body into hers, trying to get past her, knowing he had to escape her presence or lose control.

She moaned, the sound escaping from her lips as she grabbed his arm to steady herself. She felt his hard muscles tense, and loosened her grasp, letting her curved hand glide downward.

He stopped, turned and looked at her. She encircled his wrist and brought his hand up to her lips. They stood there gazing into each other's eyes while she caressed the back of his hand, savoring the texture of hairy male flesh.

Spreading his palm open, she lowered her mouth and kissed his hand. When his hand shook, she ran the tip of her tongue up and down his little finger, and, one by one, made love to each adjoining appendage.

"I'm just as afraid as you are," she said, placing his open hand at the base of her throat.

He ran his hand upward, grasped her chin and tilted her face toward his. She's right, he thought, we're both afraid of the power we have over each other.

She might have lied about loving him eighteen years ago, but the passion she'd felt had been real. Bonnie Jean had always brought out the baser, animalistic instinct in him, and he'd sworn he'd never again succumb to the primeval man she released in him.

"Are you?" he asked, running his thumb across the pad of her lower lip.

"Yes," she admitted. "I'm afraid of wanting you as badly as I once did. Afraid that you'll hurt me all over again."

He released her chin, and pulled her into his arms. "Am I something you want badly?"

Her breath caught in her throat, and for a split second she couldn't breathe. Being this close to C.J.—in his arms, their bodies touching intimately—created tremors deep within her. She threw her arms around his neck, pressing her breasts into his chest.

He cupped the side of her hip in one big hand and moved her into the cradle of his thighs. She felt his arousal and rubbed against him, wanting, needing, longing for more.

The yearning within him had been building for endless days and lonely nights. The need for a woman had been growing steadily—the desire for this particular woman had been festering inside him for eighteen years. He could have her, quench his thirst for her unique nectar, and ease the ever-present ache within him. But she had betrayed him once, broken his heart and destroyed his pride. The thought of losing control, allowing a woman like Bonnie Jean to have power over him, was something he could never allow, no matter how much he wanted to.

He ran his hands up and down her arms, then moved backward, separating their bodies. He had to put a stop to this madness. Now was neither the time nor the place, and he prayed for the strength to resist temptation in the future. He turned his head.

"C.J., please don't." She reached for him, and he pulled away. She reached for him again.

C.J. refused to look at her, even when she traced his lower lip with her fingertip and whispered his name. He noticed people coming out of the country club, his mother and Polly in the middle of a group of older ladies. Barbara Massey was conspicuously missing.

"The auction must be over. There's Mother." He took Bonnie Jean by the shoulders and shoved her backward.

When she fell against the Continental, he realized he'd pushed her much harder than he'd intended. She glared up at him when he offered his hand to assist her.

"Don't bother. You wouldn't want your mother to see you touching me." Bonnie Jean laughed, but he saw the glimmer of tears in her eyes.

"Did I hurt you?" He didn't want to hurt her, not ever. More than anything he wanted to love her, to take her in his arms and tell her that the past didn't matter, that nothing mattered but the two of them.

She laughed again, louder, and the tears escaped and ran down her cheeks into the wispy strands of hair curled about her ears.

"Would you like me to take Dorothea and Polly

home?'' Wheeler Yancey asked as he escorted both ladies to the back of C.J.'s Mercedes.

C.J. looked at Bonnie Jean. She walked away from him and past his mother.

"How are you today, Bonnie Jean?'' Polly Drew asked, reaching out to touch the girl's arm.

"Never better, Polly. You?''

"Can't say when I've had a more delightful afternoon.'' Polly giggled when she heard Dorothea gasp.

"Have you talked to Laurel recently?'' Bonnie Jean asked.

"I was just telling Wheeler and Louise that she called last night and told me she's pregnant. Isn't it wonderful? Laurel will make such a good mother.''

Bonnie Jean looked at C.J. just in time to see the color drain from his face, and suddenly regretted having asked about Laurel. Even though she'd done it deliberately to rankle C.J., she realized the unexpected news of Laurel's impending motherhood had shaken him badly.

She suspected that C.J. wanted children, and regretted that he and Kathie Lou hadn't been able to have any. If only things had been different, she could have given him a child—a daughter who would have been seventeen years old now.

"I'm ready to go, Wheeler,'' Bonnie Jean said. "I need to get to The Plantation before the dinner crowd.''

"Sure thing.'' Wheeler put his arm around Bonnie Jean and led her toward her Cadillac.

C.J. walked around the Mercedes and opened the door for his mother and Polly. Dorothea stepped inside. Polly placed her fragile hand on his, and squeezed.

"Laurel has found a happiness with John that's within your reach, Carter. Things are not always the way they seem, my boy, so don't be foolish enough to let your unbending Southern pride stand in your way."

Polly slipped inside the car beside Dorothea. C.J. looked across the country club parking area and caught a glimpse of his uncle and Bonnie Jean.

Damn! Why, after all this time, did he still want that woman so much?

Six

Gray clouds floated in the sky like sooty marshmallows, and a unseasonably warm wind whipped through the trees, sending dead leaves dancing in the air.

C.J. Moody held a mug of steaming black coffee in his right hand and the current issue of the *Observer* in his left. He quickly scanned the half-page ad announcing the grand opening of Harland's restaurant on New Year's Eve.

He smiled, tossed the paper on the nearby glass table and walked across the brick patio to the steps leading down into the backyard. Taking in a deep breath of fresh morning air, he looked out over the land, vast acres of Southern soil that had been in his mother's family for six generations. This land had gone directly from the Chickasaw Indians to Obediah Yancey, C.J.'s ancestor.

He wondered if Bonnie Jean had seen the ad. Probably not, or she'd already be beating his door down. Perhaps it was a childish gesture on his part, maybe even spiteful, but he'd be damned if he'd let her name the restaurant Sugar Hill. He knew the name change would cost them money, but he didn't care. Even though the signs and menus had been ordered, they could be reordered. He had tried everything a reasonable man could try to persuade Bonnie Jean to change the name of the restaurant, but she'd been adamant. So, he'd finally decided to take the bull by the horns.

Sometime today, she'd confront him, demand a retraction of the ad, and remind him that her contract with Yancey-Moody clearly stated that she had full authority to give their establishment a name. But, if his hunch was right, Bonnie Jean was too shrewd a businesswoman to actually take legal action against her partners over such a inconsequential matter.

Of course, if she couldn't be made to see reason, C.J. had a backup plan. And he was quite certain his compromise plan was one Bonnie Jean wouldn't be able to resist. She'd always been a risk taker, a woman willing to gamble on life in the hopes of winning big. After all, she'd traded her innocence on the chance of getting him to fall in love with her, and she'd won that bet. Then she'd bet his love for her could win her big money from his mother. And, she'd won that bet, too.

"Damn hot for this late in the year," Wheeler Yancey said as he walked through the open French doors leading out onto the patio. "Here it is after Thanksgiving and the temperature's still in the seventies."

C.J. finished his coffee and turned to face his uncle. "You can skip the weather report and say what you've come out here to say." He figured Wheeler had seen the *Observer* and was ready to take an inch off his hide for going against Bonnie Jean's wishes.

Wheeler chuckled and walked across the patio to stand beside his nephew. "God, how I love the sight! As long as I can remember, I've gotten a thrill out of just standing here looking out as far as the eye can see at this beautiful land."

"Are you trying to make a point?" C.J. asked. "Or are you simply being sentimental today?"

"This land's belonged to the Yancey family since the early 1800s."

"A fact of which I'm well aware."

"You're the last of the line, boy. The end of our little family dynasty." Wheeler placed his hand on C.J.'s shoulder. "You need children. Someone to inherit all this."

"You're a fine one to be talking. You didn't produce any offspring yourself.'

"Never married." Wheeler Yancey's smile disappeared from his rugged face. "There was a woman once, a long time ago."

"Why didn't you marry her?"

"She died. Had tuberculosis. She was always a frail little thing." Wheeler dropped his hand from C.J.'s shoulder and turned his head slightly. He wiped the moisture from his eyes and cleared his throat.

"Funny thing about us, boy, your mother and me. We loved, we lost and we never loved again."

"A family trait, I suppose." C.J. didn't want to admit that he'd never loved another woman after Bonnie Jean betrayed him. Not one woman he'd bedded, hell, not even his own wife had been able to capture his heart. He'd given it to Bonnie Jean, and whether he liked it or not, she still had it.

"You're luckier than your mother and I. The woman you love is still alive, you two just got separated for a while. All you have to do is reach out for her and she'd come running."

"Tell me something, Uncle Wheeler. Why now, after all these years, are you and Mother so determined to get me and Bonnie Jean back together, when eighteen years ago both of you were adamantly opposed to my marrying Sally Vickers's daughter?"

"Thea and I made a big mistake, son." Wheeler grunted and ran his hand across his chin. "Bonnie Jean is a fine woman. Why don't you give her a second chance? Hell, boy, give yourself a second chance."

"Neither of us wants a second chance. Whatever love I felt for her died a long time ago. And she loved me so much she took ten thousand dollars from Mother to break up with me." The very thought brought pack the pain, the anger, the deep wounds of betrayal. "She played me for a sucker, and we both know it. All the while she was professing her undying love for me, she was putting out for Bubba Harland."

"Things aren't always the way they seem, boy. Me

and your mama did what we thought was best for you eighteen years ago. We were wrong.''

"It's too late," C.J. said, and walked across the patio and into the house.

"It's never too late, boy. As long as there's life there's hope."

"All I want is to get Bonnie Jean Harland out of my life for good." C.J. stopped just inside the doorway. "Once this restaurant opens, I don't ever intend to see her again."

Bonnie Jean finished off the last bite of cornflakes and set her bowl and spoon in the sink. She poured herself another cup of coffee and sat back at the kitchen table. Rubbing her fingertips in a circular motion at her temples seemed to help her throbbing headache. She wished the aspirin she'd taken before breakfast would hurry up and relieve the pain.

Unable to sleep last night, she'd tossed and turned until after midnight, then she'd gotten out of bed, put on her favorite Patsy Cline tape and drunk two orange sodas while she tried to read a new horror book she'd just bought last week. Finally she'd put the book down and simply given in to the self-pity she'd been feeling.

Hours spent reevaluating her life had brought her to one conclusion. She still cared deeply for C.J. Moody whether she wanted to or not, and there was no doubt in her mind that the man still cared for her. Even he admitted that he wanted her. She knew they couldn't build a relationship on sex alone, but it could be a beginning. If she could put a crack in that steel-plated armor of his, they might have a chance. If only he wasn't such a stubborn fool, so unbending and unforgiving.

But did she have the guts to risk her heart again? Could she go through the pain of mistrust and rejection?

She could tell C.J. the truth about what actually happened eighteen years ago. She could tell him that their mothers had concocted a scheme to break them up—his mother wanted to see their relationship ended, her mother wanted the ten thousand dollars Dorothea had offered. Sally Vickers had enlisted Bubba Harland's help to set up the little scene C.J. had witnessed that long-ago night on Sugar Hill. Bonnie Jean had tried to tell him the truth then, but he'd refused to listen. He had accused her of being a whore just like her mother.

She didn't know when C.J. had found out about the ten thousand dollars, but Bubba had told her years later. He had been drunk and verbally abusive when he'd blurted out that C.J. Moody would never want her back so she might as well quit dreaming of him. She could still hear Bubba's slurred taunts.

"His mama told him she gave you the money, that you'd agreed to take it to break up with him. She told him a long time ago to make sure he never changed his mind about you." Bubba had glared at her with bloodshot eyes. "Who'd you think you were, anyway, running after a Moody? His mama was a Yancey, and his grandmother was a Fenner. And you don't even know who your old man was."

Even if she told C.J. that she hadn't taken Dorothea

Moody's payoff, that she'd been as much a victim as he had been, he might not believe her. And she was certain he'd never believe the truth about Bubba.

Of course, one truth would lead to another, just as one lie had led to another. Even if she could explain everything else, how could she ever tell him about his daughter? That black-haired, blue-eyed little angel he'd never had a chance to know. Would he ever forgive her for what happened to Cara Jean?

A knock at the back door brought Bonnie Jean out of her memories. She looked up to see Wheeler Yancey's smiling face in the door window. She waved, motioning him to come inside.

He opened the door and walked in. "Got a cup of coffee for an old man?"

"What are you doing here so early in the morning?" she asked, getting up to pour him some coffee.

"Brought you a copy of this week's *Observer*." He laid the paper down on the table. "C.J. ran the first ad announcing the grand opening of the restaurant."

"That's wonderful." She handed Wheeler a blue ceramic coffee mug.

"I think you should reserve your opinion until you see the ad. You might not think it's so wonderful." Wheeler sat down in a high-back pine chair.

"Uh-oh, what's he done?" Bonnie Jean sat down, picked up the *Observer* and opened it. She spread the newspaper on the table and took a long hard look at the advertisement. "That damn bas—"

"Now, now, gal. It was to be expected." Wheeler took a healthy swig from the mug. "After all, he told you how he felt about rubbing the town's nose in your success.''

"*Harland's?* He's substituted the name Harland's for the name Sugar Hill.''

"Yep.''

"He's not going to get away with this. Our contract states plainly that I get to choose the restaurant's name.''

"So it does.''

"I'll call my lawyer. I'll sue. I'll—''

"I don't think that will be necessary.''

Bonnie Jean looked up at Wheeler, her hazel eyes sparkling with the mixture of emotions whirling inside her. "He wants a confrontation, doesn't he?''

"Yep. I think he's got something up his sleeve.''

"Well, I guess it's time,'' she said, looking down at the advertisement. "We've been pushing each other pretty hard. Sooner or later, one of us is going to have to break.''

"I hope it's C.J.''

"It damn well isn't going to be me!''

Clutching a folded copy of the *Observer* in her hand, Bonnie Jean marched out of The Plantation and up the street to the newspaper office. When she entered the building, several employees spoke to her, but she ignored them and went straight to C.J.'s office.

"Ms. Harland, I'm afraid you can't go in right now,'' the attractive young secretary said. "Mr. Moody is on the phone.''

Bonnie Jean grabbed the doorknob, turned to the

young woman and smiled. "I think Mr. Moody is expecting me."

"I see. Well…er…I don't seem to have you listed in his appointment book. Perhaps, if you can wait—"

Bonnie Jean opened the door, walked in and closed the door in the secretary's face. She had every intention of using the newspaper she held to knock some sense into C.J. Moody.

He sat with his back to her, the phone clutched in his hand as he mumbled softly. His navy jacket hung over the back of the chair.

"I'm sorry, Mr. Moody, but Ms. Harland wouldn't wait to be announced." The secretary entered the room and eyed Bonnie Jean with disgust.

Slowly, very slowly, he turned around in his swivel chair and looked at Bonnie Jean. The top button of his white shirt was undone, his red and navy tie slightly loosened. He smiled at her before looking at his secretary.

"It's all right, Allie. I'll take care of Ms. Harland."

The young woman nodded, gave Bonnie Jean one last disapproving glance and left the room. C.J. continued his conversation, completely ignoring his visitor. She walked across the room and stood looking out the windows that faced Main Street. Tuscumbia epitomized small Southern towns, the mixture of old and new evident in the architecture. She loved this town with its elegant courthouse, its stately old homes and its warm and friendly people. Of course, Tuscumbia did have its share of society snobs.

The longer Bonnie Jean waited, the angrier she became. He'd promised her a war, and it seemed that he had every intention of keeping that promise. She'd expected the advertisement, but not the name change. She couldn't believe that C.J. had disregarded her opinion entirely and named her new restaurant Harland's. And why? Because he knew how much it meant to her to call it Sugar Hill? Or was it to punish her for being both the woman he desired and despised?

She clutched the newspaper in her hand and continuously swatted her open palm. The crisp popping sound echoed in the quiet office. She paced back and forth in front of his desk, occasionally cutting her eyes to catch a glimpse of the big man sitting behind the desk.

Her patience exhausted, Bonnie Jean leaned over the front of his desk and pointed the paper right in his face. "Dammit, C.J., tell them to call you later!"

He'd kept her cooling her heels long enough. She should have called her lawyer and sued him. She could still do that. Damn C.J.'s contrary hide.

"Lunch tomorrow, then," he said and put the receiver down. "What can I do for you, Ms. Harland?"

"Don't you Ms. Harland me, you sorry, no-good—"

"Such language. People will suspect you're not a lady."

Bonnie Jean blasted him with a few choice words of what those people could do and exactly where C.J. could go. She waved the paper under his nose. "I want you to print a retraction. I want a whole new ad."

C.J. picked up his coffee mug and leaned back in his chair. "Or what?"

Still clutching the newspaper in her fist, she drew back and looked at him. "Or what? Or I'll sue you, that's what."

"Have you talked to your lawyer?"

"Well, no. But that's my next stop."

"He'll tell you that it's best to settle this thing with me personally. After all I am, or rather Yancey-Moody is, your business partner in this restaurant. I simply prefer Harland's instead of Sugar Hill as a name for our new establishment." He lifted the mug to his lips and finished off the last drops of lukewarm coffee.

"You're not fighting fair, running that full-page ad announcing the wrong name for my restaurant."

"You've never fought fair, Bonnie Jean. Why should I?"

"Because you're supposed to be a Southern gentleman."

"Oh, I'm that all right. I'm a Southern gentleman if nothing else. Just ask my mother. But I would have thought Uncle Wheeler had taught you that Southern gentlemen have their own code of ethics, and winning is a number one priority." He waved his hand, and the morning sunlight reflected off the heavy gold antique ring he wore on his right ring finger. "But I have a proposition for you, Ms. Harland. I could be persuaded to allow you to use the name you want for your restaurant."

She threw the newspaper down on his desk like a gauntlet, for she knew he was going to offer her a challenge—a duel to the death. She laughed silently, a wicked little grin curling the corners of her mouth.

He stood and walked around his desk to within a few feet of her. God, she smelled good. Like fresh air and sunshine. And a delicate hint of bacon, eggs and strong coffee clung to her. She'd come straight from The Plantation, no doubt.

"What sort of proposition?" she asked.

"You used to be pretty good at playing pool."

"So?"

"So, how about a little bet?"

She eyed him suspiciously. "You want the two of us to play pool, the way we used to? And you want us to make a bet?"

"That's right."

She moved toward him, stopped only a few inches away, and placed her hands on her hips. He looked at her then and noticed how demurely she was dressed. He'd never really thought about it, but she always dressed that way. She wore a calf-length tan skirt, a beige silk blouse, and tortoiseshell earrings and bracelet. She looked like the lady she had once so desperately wanted to be.

He'd known she would come storming into his office the minute she saw the ad. He'd actually been looking forward to this confrontation. He could have taken her to court about the restaurant's name, but he didn't see the point. He supposed it was foolish to relish the idea of playing pool with her again. In an odd sort of way, he hoped that returning to the past on a brief visit might be just the thing to release him from his obsession with Bonnie Jean. If he could get her to agree to go to Cody's for their pool game, back to a place he'd shared with Bonnie Jean Vickers when he'd been so in love with her, he'd probably realize that she hadn't changed—that she was still the money-hungry little whore from Sugar Hill. She should look right at home in that smoky, sleazy poolroom. Once he'd seen her in the proper setting, he figured he could rid himself of her memory once and for all. And have a little fun while he was doing it.

His life hadn't had much fun in it, not for years, and he had discovered—thanks to Bonnie Jean, he freely admitted—that he missed a little of the carefree pleasures he'd once known.

"What sort of bet do you have in mind?" she asked.

"I remember that you're almost as good a pool player as I am. So, let's play for who gets to name our restaurant. I win, it's Harland's. You win, it's Sugar Hill."

"A pool game?"

"That's right, or perhaps several games."

She simply didn't understand why C.J. was offering her a chance to beat him at a game they'd often enjoyed playing when they'd been dating. He knew she was a good player, and had beaten him several times. What he didn't know was that she'd never given up the game, and her skills were sharper than ever. "Maybe you should ask Wheeler about the pool games we've played at my place. I have a pool table in my garage."

"You know that Wheeler taught me to play when I was a kid. We've got a pool table at the house and we play several times a week. I'm good, honey. Better than Wheeler.'' He knew his uncle was an excellent player, and that's why he doubted Bonnie Jean had won many times when she'd played the old man. Wheeler had probably let her win.

"I'm pretty good myself, or have you forgotten?"

"I haven't forgotten," he said. "What do you suggest? Eight ball? Rotation?"

"Straight pool." She watched his eyes widen in surprise, and licked her lips, already feeling a sense of satisfaction. "We could play at my place, in the garage."

"We could play at my house, too, but we aren't. If we play, we'll play at Cody's. Tonight." He enjoyed watching her reaction at the mention of Cody's Poolroom.

It figures, she thought. He wants us to play at the local pool hall with a dozen rednecks watching. There was more to this game than C.J. was admitting. She knew he must have some ulterior motive for wanting to take them back to Cody's, where they'd often gone on their dates. Well, he definitely wanted his pound of flesh before giving up the fight.

"Agreed," she said. "You win, it's Harland's. I win, it's Sugar Hill. But you can go ahead and get the ad ready for next week's paper announcing the grand opening of Sugar Hill on New Year's Eve because I'm going to beat you, Mr. Moody." In a casual yet sultry motion, she put her arms around his neck, and rubbed his nose with her own.

She's playing some sort of game, he thought, and

reminded himself that she couldn't be trusted. "You don't mind playing at Cody's?"

"I have a lot of good memories there." She closed her eyes and nuzzled her face against his neck.

"Bonnie Jean, what are you up to?" He put his hands at her waist and nudged her backward.

She clung to him, tightening her hold around his neck. "What makes you think I'm up to anything? You're the one who suggested the pool game, and it's your idea that we play at Cody's."

Still holding her waist, he jerked her up against him, and glared down into her sparkling eyes. "I didn't think you'd want to play at Cody's."

"Why not?"

"It doesn't exactly fit your new ladylike image."

"Is that what this is all about?" Leaving one arm draped around his neck, she reached down and took his hand, rubbing her thumb in circles over the palm. "You want to put me in my place, so to speak."

"And just where is your place?"

"Obviously, you think it's at Cody's."

"You used to fit in there quite well."

"So did you." Bonnie Jean leaned closer, her lips almost touching his ear. "It's not going to work," she whispered.

"What?" C.J. pushed her away, squinting as his gaze focused on her face.

She turned around and walked toward the outer door. After opening the door, she stopped, her back still to him. "No matter what happens at Cody's tonight, you're still going to want me...probably even more than you do now."

* * *

Hank Williams Jr.'s "All My Rowdy Friends Are Coming Over Tonight" blared from the radio sitting on a shelf behind the bar. Cigar and cigarette smoke filled the air, mingling with the music, loud talk and hearty laughter.

Bonnie Jean leaned back in her chair and casually glanced toward the entrance. She checked her watch, saw that it was five till seven and knew C.J. would be here any minute. Being a gentleman, he was never late for an appointment.

"Guess I'd better get going," Elaine Harland said as she stood. "I can't believe he asked you to come here."

Bonnie Jean stood, put her arm around Elaine's waist and hugged her. "I never realized how sleazy this place was when C.J. used to bring me here. Of course, I would have gone anywhere with him, even hell, and thought it was wonderful."

"Good luck. I hope you win." Elaine smiled and winked at Bonnie Jean. "In more ways than one."

"C.J.'s a good player, but so am I."

"Don't forget to make that side bet," Elaine said, and turned to leave.

"I'll keep it in mind."

Bonnie Jean waved goodbye to her sister-in-law, thankful that Elaine had agreed to come with her. It had been years since she'd been inside Cody's, but it hadn't changed much. A pool hall was a pool hall. Trying to avoid all the curious glances from the male patrons, she walked across the room, pausing to watch a pool game already in progress. Nervously she checked her watch again.

Had she been a fool to agree to meet C.J. here? They could easily have played at her house or his. It was obvious he'd insisted they play here for reasons only he knew, but she had a pretty good idea what his ulterior motive was. She had spent eighteen years fighting a long, hard battle to overcome her past, to rise above her legacy of poverty and illegitimacy. Did C.J. want to drag her back down into the mire from which she'd come? Did he think subjecting her to this sleazy atmosphere would make it easier for him to reject her? If he had to see her at Cody's to remind him that she wasn't a *lady,* then Bonnie Jean knew she must be getting through to him, and hopefully others as well. If she could get C.J. Moody to change his narrow-minded, unforgiving attitude, then there was hope that the whole town would see her in a new light.

She turned around just in time to see C.J. enter. He moved into Cody's Poolroom at a slow, steady pace, acknowledging a few friendly hellos from several acquaintances. Everyone in town knew Carter Jackson Moody IV. Tonight he wore tan corduroy slacks and a navy turtleneck pullover and, as always, looked like a model just stepping from the cover of *GQ*. His thick salt-and-pepper hair gleamed silver in the muted lighting, and his dark mustache appeared almost black.

Bonnie Jean wondered if she'd ever live to see the day that C.J. didn't arouse every elemental female need within her. Just the sight of him sent shivers through her body and warmed her quivering insides.

C.J. watched her walk over to the third pool table

and run her hand across the green felt surface. Even though she looked every inch a lady, and totally out of place at Cody's, there was something earthy and primitive about Bonnie Jean. There was a sultry, sensual air about her. The way she looked—long shapely legs, round firm breasts, mesmerizing hazel eyes and a soft kissable mouth. The way she moved—her hips swaying, her whole body in tune to some ancient sexual rhythm. The way she talked—that husky, throaty voice, that deep, womanly laugh.

C.J. saw her caressing the pool table, her white-blond hair brushing across the foot rail, and damned himself for a fool. Just looking at her made him hard with need. No other woman had ever had such a strong effect on him. In eighteen years he'd never again known the passion he'd shared with Bonnie Jean.

Her black tailored slacks were clenched at her tiny waist with a wide macramé belt of black, gold, silver and bronze. A small black bow held part of her shoulder-length hair away from her face, while curly tendrils fell across her forehead and caressed her cheeks. The long-sleeved blouse she wore was a bronze silk, and although it was rather loose, it didn't disguise the fullness of her breasts or the brevity of her waist.

He looked around and saw an accumulation of men of various ages and sizes. The other two tables were occupied with players. Half a dozen or so roughnecks sat around guzzling beer and ogling the only two females on the premises, Tara Dumars, the young waitress, and Bonnie Jean. One man stood at the bar talking with Cody, the burly redhead who managed the place.

C.J. walked across the room, opened his case and took out his cue. "Straight pool?"

"Straight pool." She took her cue from its case, joined the two pieces, and ran a loving hand down the length of the wooden surface. She'd had the cue custom-made several years ago, and she never played without it. "No need to prolong your agony. How about best three out of five?"

"Fine with me."

"About our bet. You win, our restaurant is Harland's. I win, the name is Sugar Hill." She motioned for Cody to rack the balls.

C.J. nodded and watched while Cody racked the fifteen balls. If he lost this game and she called the restaurant Sugar Hill, he could well imagine the town's reaction. Some would be amused, others outraged.

"What about a little side bet?" she asked, brushing chalk on the tip of her cue with light side-to-side strokes. She'd given the side bet a lot of thought. She wasn't sure why it was so important to her, but it was. If she won, he'd have to fulfill a promise he'd made her long ago.

"I don't see that any side bets are necessary."

"No, they're not necessary, but they should make the outcome more interesting. Naming the restaurant is just a matter of one of us getting our own way, but a side bet should be something special. Something no one else would give us, and something we couldn't get for ourselves."

"What do you have in mind?"

"If I win, I want a date with you." She laid the chalk down, exposed side up. "I want to be your date for Dorothea's annual Christmas Eve party."

"What?"

"Eighteen years ago you promised to take me to your mother's Christmas party as your bride." She looked over at C.J. wondering exactly what memories her words had evoked, but his face was blank of any emotion. "But we didn't quite make it to Christmas. By then you were already overseas on an assignment and I had married Bubba and moved to Nashville."

"And you were pregnant with your lover's child."

"Yes."

Damn her, he thought. She talked about their past as if it didn't cause her the least bit of pain, as if the fact that she'd betrayed him had never bothered her conscience. "You want to hobnob with Dorothea Moody's socially prominent friends?"

"I want to spend Christmas with you at your home." Not one Christmas had passed without her thinking about spending it with C.J., about what it would have been like if she'd had enough self-confidence at eighteen to stand up to him and make him understand the truth, that she hadn't betrayed him, that she loved only him and would for the rest of her life.

"If I agree to this side bet, what do I get if I win?"

"What do you want?" she asked. "What's the one thing I can give you that no one else can?"

He chalked his cue and without looking at her said,

"I want you in my bed for one night. And then I never want to see you again."

She burst into laughter, and looked up to catch him staring at her breasts. C.J. moved his eyes upward to her face, and she realized that he wasn't joking. Suddenly she felt as if he'd slapped her. Did he really think that venting his sexual frustration on her would rid him of his desire for her? Didn't he realize that the attraction they felt for each other could never be permanently sated?

Without blinking an eye, she stared directly at him. "It's a deal."

Damn her! Damn her a million times over, he said to himself. He hadn't actually thought she'd agree to such an outrageous suggestion. "We've made our bets," he said. "Now let's see who wins."

They each placed a ball behind the head string, banked it off the foot rail, and watched the balls move forward. Bonnie Jean's stopped the closest to the head rail, and she opted to shoot first.

She gripped the cue lightly but firmly with her thumb and forefinger, forming a bridge with the fingers of her left hand. She positioned the cue tip close to the cue ball and pulled the trigger.

C.J. forced himself to take his eyes off her curvy backside and concentrate on the game. Allowing her sexy body to distract him could cost him the game, and ultimately a great deal more.

He watched as her shot clipped the corner ball, sending the cueball off three rails. The two-ball hit the end rail softly and the five-ball hit the side rail and returned to the pack. C.J. realized he'd have at least six feet of green to cover if he tried to score.

Bonnie Jean stepped back, smiling as she stood waiting for C.J. to shoot. He chalked his cue, called his shot and proceeded.

The games went well for her, mainly because she was the better player, but also because C.J. often lost his patience and tried several extremely difficult shots more than once. C.J. won the third game, and by that time, they had acquired a crowd of onlookers.

C.J. started the fourth game, executing the opening shot perfectly. He knew he had to win this game to stay alive. She's a damned hustler, he thought, then revised his opinion. No, she was one hell of a player, and she was going to win if he didn't play better than he'd ever played in his life. God, he'd been a fool to make such a stupid bet with her. This would teach him to never underestimate Bonnie Jean Harland. Even though he thought nothing she did would surprise him, she was constantly doing just that—surprising him. He found himself wishing he could get to know her better, then cursed himself for an idiot. This woman was bad news.

Bonnie Jean looked the situation over. She weighed her options, then lagged the cue ball to the rear of the pack. It cost her a point, but it was better than taking the chance of leaving a makable shot by hitting the pack hard enough to drive a ball to the rail.

Despite playing her best, she lost the fourth game. She knew it was partly due to the fact she hadn't played with C.J. in years and had forgotten how distracting his presence could be. She watched his every move, noticing the way his muscles flexed beneath his shirt, the way his hips curved, the way he smiled and frowned and contemplated the next shot. She noticed the dots of perspiration form on his forehead and wanted to wipe them away. And when she wasn't watching him, she could feel his gaze on her. It was as if he were memorizing every curve, and she wondered if he was comparing her thirty-six-year-old body to the one he'd touched and kissed and adored eighteen years ago.

During the short lull before the fifth and final game, the buxom Tara came up to C.J., brushing against him and grinning. "Aren't you thirsty, sweetie?"

"Why don't you bring us both a cold beer?" Bonnie Jean said, hating the way the woman was flirting with C.J. She wanted to jerk the woman by the hair of her bleached head.

"After you win this game, why don't you stick around? This is a weeknight and the place closes at ten," the waitress said. "You could drive me home."

C.J. looked at the woman. The girl was young enough to be his daughter. But he noticed the malevolent stare Bonnie Jean aimed at him, and smiled at the waitress. "I'll keep that in mind."

"Hurry up with those beers," Bonnie Jean said. C.J. would not be leaving with that female, she thought, even if she had to knock him unconscious and drive him home herself. And he was not going to win this game. She had too much riding on the outcome—her future and perhaps C.J.'s.

Cody racked the balls for the final game. Everyone in the poolroom watched as C.J. opened and failed to drive two balls and the cue ball to a rail. He looked at Bonnie Jean to see if she intended to take the shot or have the balls reracked. She chalked her cue, bent over the table, and aimed.

She called her shot, succeeded, and relished the cheers from the roughnecks. She realized C.J. felt the pressure more and more with each shot as she outplayed him again and again.

The game ended in triumph for Bonnie Jean and defeat for C.J. The crowd applauded her win, and the blond waitress tried to comfort him in his loss. Bonnie Jean laid her cue on the table. She'd won, and she should have felt heady with victory, but she didn't. Her restaurant would be named Sugar Hill, and she would finally share Christmas with C.J. at his family's home. Eighteen years ago he had made her promises that he'd never kept, promises of love that would last a lifetime. It might seem foolish to others that she wanted this one promise kept, but to Bonnie Jean it held a significance no one else could possibly understand.

She watched as C.J. thwarted the young waitress's advances. He grabbed the beer mug and finished off the remaining liquid.

"Congratulations," he said, looking at her across the pool table. "You're an awfully good player. I underestimated you…something I'll never do again."

"Thanks. You're a pretty good player yourself."

He took his cue apart and put it away. His hands were steady, but his heartbeat accelerated when she came around the table and extended her hand. He looked at her outstretched hand for a few minutes before taking it in his. They exchanged a hearty hand-shake, but when he started to release her hand, she held fast.

"I promise you won't be sorry you lost." She moved closer, still clutching his hand.

"I regretted this whole thing before I ever got here tonight." He wanted nothing more than to take her in his arms, shake her soundly and then kiss the breath out of her.

"Give me a chance, C.J." She looked up at him, her eyes misty, hopes and dreams and desire shining in their golden-green depths.

"Don't hold me to our side bet." He grabbed her by the shoulders, uncaring that several patrons still watched the two of them.

She threw her arms around his neck and, standing on tiptoe, whispered, "I was the best thing that ever happened to you." And then she kissed him.

Stunned, he didn't respond at first. When she ran the tip of her tongue over his lips in a circular motion, he pulled her into his arms and returned the kiss full-force. Damn, he wanted her. Wanted her badly, and now.

Catcalls and whistles ended the kiss. C.J. pulled away and stared at her, his eyes filled with the fury of a man denied release, and the rage of a man feeling like a fool.

"C.J.?" She reached for him.

"I'll pick you up at seven o'clock on Christmas Eve. Dress is formal. Until then, I don't want to see you." He picked up his case, turned around and walked to the front door, not once looking back, not even when she called his name again. The sound of the door slamming echoed in her ears. She bit her lip trying not to cry.

Now's not the time for tears, she told herself. He'll cool off, and things will work out. They had to. Finally Bonnie Jean admitted to herself that she'd never stopped loving C.J. and that, even though she was afraid of being hurt all over again, she did want a second chance with him.

Christmas was a magical time of year. A time for hopes and dreams to come true. A season of miracles. Perhaps, she and C.J. would receive a miracle. Lord knew, they were long overdue.

Seven

Carter Moody draped the bow tie around his neck and knotted it with expertise. He slipped into his black evening jacket and turned to face the mirror. Running his hand over his cleanly shaven jaw, he inspected his reflection.

Well, what do you see, Moody? he asked himself. The physical image showed a tall, muscular man in his prime. A man of obvious wealth and breeding. But the man inside was what C.J. sought, the man who'd long ago lost the ability to feel love. Bonnie Jean had done that to him. No, that wasn't true. He'd done it to himself. He had allowed her betrayal to fester inside him like an unhealed wound. The only way he had been able to deal with the love that wouldn't die was to turn that love into hatred.

He had been able to keep up the pretense for

years—as long as he didn't have to see her, he was safe. But she'd changed all that when she'd come home to Tuscumbia four years ago. And in the few months since Yancey-Moody had gone into business with Ms. Harland, the woman had wreaked havoc with his emotions. He couldn't be in the same room with her without wanting her, without longing to ease her clothes from her luscious body and bury himself deep inside her.

Would she be willing to give him what he wanted? It was obvious she was as hot for him as he was for her. But what would be the outcome of their love-making? She'd want a commitment. She'd want love. He couldn't—wouldn't—risk either. If he gave her what she wanted and she betrayed him again, he wouldn't be able to survive.

C.J.'s bedroom door opened, and Dorothea Moody waltzed in, a string of pearls in her hand.

"Could you help me with these, dear?" Dorothea asked.

C.J. took the necklace and circled his mother's neck with the pearls. "You look lovely tonight."

"Thank you, Carter. You look handsome as always."

"You haven't said much about tonight's special guest." C.J. had been puzzled by his mother's attitude when he'd told her that Bonnie Jean Harland would be attending their annual Christmas Eve party. She'd simply smiled and told him that any friend of his was always welcome.

"That's one of the reasons I'm here now," Dorothea admitted, turning to inspect her appearance in the mirror. "I've given this a great deal of thought. I've discussed the matter at great length with Wheeler."

C.J. noticed how tense his mother seemed, and a knot of apprehension formed in the pit of his stomach. "What are you talking about?" he asked.

"I was wrong about Bonnie Jean." Dorothea's voice quivered. She cleared her throat and turned to face her son.

"In what way were you wrong, Mother?" He couldn't believe what he'd just heard. Dorothea Yancey Moody never admitted when she was wrong. Mainly because she never thought she was.

"I didn't believe Bonnie Jean was the right girl for you."

"You weren't wrong about that." C.J. picked up his gold Rolex and antique ring from atop his dresser and put them on. "She was Bubba Harland's girl, not mine."

"I—I don't really know all the details of her relationship with her late husband, but I truly believe there was nothing more than friendship between them until after you two...ended your...your engagement."

C.J. felt a growing sense of fear. His mother was defending Bonnie Jean. There was something wrong with this scenario, something awfully wrong. "Are you forgetting that she came to you and offered to end our relationship if you'd pay her ten thousand dollars? I haven't. I'm the one who found her with Bubba, the one who got a knife in the gut."

Dorothea stiffened, and all color drained from her

face. "Bonnie Jean didn't come to me. She never knew about the money. I went to Sally Vickers."

"What are you saying?"

"I offered Sally the money if she'd find a way to break up you and Bonnie Jean."

"You told me Bonnie Jean asked for the money."

"I lied."

C.J. grabbed his mother by the shoulders and glared down at her pale face. Tears glistened in her eyes. "Tell me what the hell you're talking about."

"You know as well as I do that Bonnie Jean was very insecure, which is understandable considering her background. She never thought she was good enough for you." Dorothea paused, wiped the moisture from her cheeks, and lowered her eyes.

C.J. loosened his hold on her shoulders and took her trembling hands into his strong, steady grasp.

"She loved you," Dorothea said.

"My God, Mother, why?"

"I thought a marriage between the two of you would be hopeless. I was convinced that you should be free to make a life with a woman worthy of you."

C.J. squeezed his mother's hands tightly, then let them go. "What about Bubba?"

"Having Bubba there that night was Sally Vickers's idea." She straightened her back, tilted her head up and looked at her son, honesty brightening her eyes. "Sally knew you'd never forgive Bonnie Jean if you thought she'd betrayed you with another man."

C.J. felt pressure building inside his head, and a throbbing roar dulled every other sound. His mother's voice rumbled in his ears like thunder, and the sound

of his own heartbeat drummed as loudly as a march-
ing band. All these years, he'd hated the wrong
woman. Bonnie Jean had loved him. She hadn't betrayed him.

"Bonnie Jean never knew about the money?" C.J.
asked, admitting the truth to himself before his mother
replied.

"No, not for years. She told Wheeler that Bubba
explained things to her one night when he'd been
drinking heavily."

"Why did Bonnie Jean run off to Nashville and
marry Bubba if there was nothing going on between
them?"

"Only Bonnie Jean can answer that."

"Why, Mother, after all this time, did you decide
to tell me the truth?" And why, he wondered, had
Bonnie Jean never explained what had happened all
those years ago? Why hadn't she told him what his
mother had done? What her own mother had done?

"I love you, and I want to see you happy." Dorothea reached out and ran her trembling fingers
across C.J.'s cheek. "And I've finally realized that
you can never be truly happy without Bonnie Jean."

"I should have known he wouldn't pick me up,"
Bonnie Jean said. "I guess I should be grateful he
sent you instead of a taxi."

Wheeler Yancey maneuvered the sleek, black Corvette along Highway 72. His tall, robust body seemed
huge within the confines of the small sports car. "C.J.
was acting mighty peculiar. He came into my room,
asked me to pick you up, and then he disappeared.

Thea said he went out, but she didn't know where. When I tried to question her, she wouldn't say a word.''

"Do you suppose C.J. and his mother argued about me?"

"I doubt that. I told you that Thea is coming around where you're concerned."

"Maybe this is a mistake," Bonnie Jean said. "I don't belong at Dorothea Moody's Christmas Eve party any more than I belong with her son."

"Well, gal, who knows?" Wheeler turned off the highway and onto the side road that led to the Yancey mansion. "I thought C.J. would've given in by now and admitted he still loves you. Of course, he's a stubborn cuss."

"You could be wrong, you know."

"No, I'm not. He loves you all right, and wants you something fierce. The same way you love and want him."

Bonnie Jean sipped on her second glass of ginger ale and tried her best to take part in the conversation. Polly Drew, dear lady that she was, had taken Bonnie Jean under her wing immediately after her arrival. Once the shocked expressions had worn off the guests' faces and the startled murmurs had died down, Dorothea Moody had greeted Bonnie Jean, welcoming her with genuine warmth.

There were at least twenty people milling around in the foyer and front parlor, and perhaps a dozen more circled the elegant buffet in the dining room. Several of the younger couples were dancing in the back parlor where a small combo played a cool jazz tune. But Carter Jackson Moody was conspicuously absent.

Wheeler had his arm draped around Teenie Jeffreys's shoulder while he talked with Eugene Drew, Polly's nephew. Eugene's wife, Gertrude, nibbled on the liver pâté while she gazed across the room. Bonnie Jean could feel the woman looking at her, but when she glanced across the room, Gertrude lifted her head, stuck her aristocratic nose in the air and turned away.

"I'm so excited about the grand opening of Sugar Hill," Polly Drew said. "Harvey has promised that we'll dance the night away."

"You must be so proud of your new restaurant," Clintelle Simpson said.

"What? Uh…yes. I'm…that is…we're quite proud of Sugar Hill. We're completely booked for New Year's Eve." Bonnie Jean could feel the cold, curious stares, and knew Dorothea Moody's other guests were wondering why Sally Vickers's daughter had been invited to one of *the* parties of the season.

"Hope the weather stays good for you," Peter Simpson said, then downed his rum and cola. "Heard on the weather forecast that we might get some sleet tonight. By New Year's we could be iced in."

"Oh, pooh." Clintelle playfully swatted her husband on the arm. "We don't usually get bad weather until late January or February. You shouldn't be worrying this girl about the weather. She'll have enough problems on opening night."

"Well, would you look at that," Polly said, staring out into the foyer.

"About time that boy showed up," Harvey Grimes said.

The man who stood in the foyer removing his overcoat gained all Bonnie Jean's attention. He looked magnificent in his tailored evening clothes, immaculate, and every inch the suave Southern gentleman. Only the drops of moisture clinging to his hair suggested he'd been out in the rain.

"Wonder where he's been?" Clintelle slipped her arm around her husband's. "Let's make our way over there and ask."

"I don't think you need to do that," Polly said. "Looks like Carter is coming over here."

Every muscle in Bonnie Jean's body tensed. She watched him walk into the room, ignoring all the intense stares and vocal greetings. He looked directly at her, his pale blue eyes locking on to her and holding her in a trance.

"Well, well, well." Polly Drew smiled.

Barbara Massey slunk up to C.J. and placed her arm around his waist. Halfway across the room, Bonnie Jean heard her syrupy voice say, "Why, Carter, darling, where have you been? I've been so bored without you."

Bonnie Jean tried to look away, but couldn't. She'd never hated Barbara Merritt Massey more than she did at this moment.

C.J. turned to the clinging vine who'd attached herself to him and gave her a chilling look. "Let go, Barbara, I've kept my date waiting long enough."

A hush fell over the crowd in the Yancey front parlor as Carter Jackson Moody IV rudely extracted himself from Barbara Massey's clutches. People moved aside as he walked past, never once taking his eyes off Bonnie Jean Harland. The steady beat of drums blended with the haunting moan of a saxophone as the combo in the back parlor improvised on an old Duke Ellington tune. The clink of cocktail glasses blended with the music and laughter coming from the other room.

C.J. stopped directly in front of Bonnie Jean. He held out his hand. For one endless moment she simply stared at him, then she looked down at his hand. Without saying a word, she reached out and placed her hand in his. He pulled her to his side and slipped his arm around her waist. Leaning his head down close to her ear, he whispered, "You look beautiful tonight."

Her heart raced wildly, and warmth suffused her body. She opened her mouth to tell him how handsome he looked, but couldn't get the words past her throat. The subtle scent of C.J.'s elusive cologne lingered in the air, and she breathed deeply, savoring the hint of musky masculinity that was C.J.'s alone.

With the ease of a man long used to doing things his own way, C.J. led her to the back parlor and maneuvered her through a small group of couples dancing to the bluesy tune.

She went into his arms willingly, not questioning him, although she couldn't help but wonder where he had been and why he was late for his mother's party. And even more puzzling was his attentive manner toward her since he'd entered the house. It was as if he were glad to see her, as if he'd been waiting eagerly to take her into his arms.

C.J. brought her up against him, her breasts pressed against his dark jacket. The seductive melody encouraged the intimate contact of their bodies in a slow, sensuous dance. Bonnie Jean couldn't believe he was holding her this way, with such tender passion, but neither of them could deny the effect their closeness was creating. He was hardness to her melting softness. With dreamy eyes, she gazed up at him and what she saw startled her. His eyes blazed with desire—hot, unsated longing.

"C.J.?" Her voice was a mere whisper.

He smiled down at her, and moved one hand along the length of her back, resting it just below her waist. "I remember the first time I ever danced with you."

"My senior prom." She never forgot that night, but she'd wondered if C.J. had. It had been their third date, the April before his college graduation.

"You were a pretty girl," he said, "but you're even lovelier now."

"Your being awfully nice to me, C.J." She looked at him in time to catch a hint of a smile cross his face. "Dare I hope you've had a change of heart where I'm concerned?"

He glanced down the long, creamy column of her throat to her satiny shoulders and the soft, smooth slopes of her breasts where the bodice of her dress crisscrossed. "I'll never have a change of heart where you're concerned."

He felt her tense and knew she'd misunderstood

the meaning of his words. Without any explanation, he held her closer and touched the top of her head with his lips. There was still a great deal he didn't know about what happened between them eighteen years ago, but one thing he knew for certain—he cared for Bonnie Jean. And after his mother's belated confession, he realized it was long past time to give himself and the only woman he'd ever loved a second chance at finding happiness.

He'd spent several hours driving around in the rain tonight, trying to come to terms with what his mother had told him about the past. Bonnie Jean had never asked for the money, and in the end, her mother had gotten the ten thousand dollars. Damn, why had Bonnie Jean been so naive? If only she had explained to him how inadequate she'd felt, he would have soothed all her fears and uncertainties. He could have convinced her that she was the only woman in the world for him, and always would be.

He kissed her temple, his lips brushing against her pale blond hair. She wore it up, and tiny, loose tendrils framed her face, like spun-satin moonbeams. Her dress draped her body, the winter-white silk cinched at the waist and clung to her hips. Teardrop pearls hung from her ears. The simplicity of her outfit gave her an elegance far and above any other woman in the room. She looked like a classy lady. His classy lady.

They moved in perfect rhythm to the music, his big body unbelievably graceful as he guided her steps. "You smell like exotic flowers and sweet spices," he murmured, leading her into a slow turn.

She shivered, every nerve in her body reacting to the unexpected eroticism of his words. It was as if she were dreaming, that sometime tonight between the moment C.J. entered the foyer and the moment he took her into his arms, they had entered a fantasy world. "It's my perfume," she said, her voice trembling.

"Perhaps." He dropped his hand an inch, allowing it to rest in the hollow between her waist and hips. "But whatever the scent, it has me drugged."

What could she say? She had longed for this moment, this precious moment when C.J. would treat her with respect and tenderness. She looked up into his smiling face. There was no hatred, no disgust, only the pure, sweet glow of desire.

"I've been a fool, Bonnie Jean." His deep voice was like strong brandy, intoxicating her, turning her into liquid fire.

Her body became rigid. She stopped moving, forcing him to stand still beside her on the dance floor. Out of the corner of his eyes, C.J. could see several people staring at them.

"We're becoming the center of attention," he warned.

"I'm sorry, but...perhaps you should let me go." She pulled away, only to be restrained by his arms holding her snugly against him.

"We were only dancing."

"It wasn't the dancing. It was what you were saying." She pulled back again and this time he released her.

When she walked away from him, he followed her

out of the back parlor and into the dining room. With nervous fingers she picked up a plate and moved along the buffet table, filling the dish to overflowing with a variety of edible delights. C.J. presented her with a glass of champagne.

"You must be hungry," he said, eyeing the collection of goodies on her plate.

"Yes. No." She tried to walk around him into the front parlor where she saw Wheeler talking to Polly Drew, but C.J. blocked her path.

"It's crowded in there." He nodded toward the room across the hall. "Let me take you someplace quiet and private where we can talk."

"Talk?" Yes, she thought, we need to talk. *I've got at least two dozen questions to ask you about your behavior tonight.*

He took her by the arm and led her out into the foyer and down the hallway. Every room they passed seemed to be filled with people eating, talking and dancing. When they entered Wheeler's study, they caught a middle-aged couple in a rather heated kiss. Realizing they'd been seen in a compromising situation, the red-faced pair made a hasty exit.

"I wonder if Harriet Brady is aware her husband and her sister are involved." C.J. laughed and pulled Bonnie Jean outside into the hallway again.

"That was embarrassing."

"For them more than for us," he said and tugged her along toward the back of the house. Opening the curtained double French doors, he led her inside a darkened room and closed the doors behind them, then took her plate and glass.

"Where are we?" she asked, blinking her eyes, trying to see in the dimly lighted room.

After setting her food and champagne on a small wicker table, he pulled her back against him, put his arms around her waist and rested his chin on top of her head. "Take a look."

She didn't dare allow herself to relax in his arms, no matter how much she wanted to. C.J. was acting very strangely. She glanced around the room and realized that three of the walls were glass and the only illumination in the dark room came from two gaslit lampposts outside the house. The noisy clatter and hum of music from the rest of the house seemed far away, like a distant echo. Outside, the rain had turned to light sleet, and the chink of frozen water hit the glass walls, creating a musical background.

"We're in Mother's sun room," he said.

"Oh."

He kissed her neck so quickly that the intimacy startled her, and she jerked away from him.

He reached out and caught her by the hand. "Now who's running from whom?" he asked in a teasing tone.

"C.J., have you been drinking?" The man was acting as if he wanted nothing more in the world than to be alone with her, and Bonnie Jean knew something had to be wrong with him.

"I told you that I'm drunk on that sweet spicy, flowery scent of yours." He encircled her waist with his big hands and dragged her up against him.

She felt his straining erection and gasped. "You... you..."

"I'm aroused," he admitted, moving his hands downward to clutch her hips and rub her body against his. "And if I don't kiss you soon, I'm going to die."

"What?" She was barely able to get the word out of her mouth before he took her lips with fierce possession. His tongue plunged inside and ravaged with such a thoroughness, Bonnie Jean instantly responded, her own tongue quickly learning his rhythm. He kneaded her buttocks through the silky material of her evening gown. Releasing her mouth, he took several deep breaths before nipping at her lips, then pampering the love-bites with the tip of his tongue. His loving attention moved slowly, savoring the taste of her flesh over her chin, across her jaw and down her smooth neck.

"Yes," she moaned.

"More?" he mumbled against her neck and raised his head. His lips moved up over her chin and her cheek until he captured her mouth once again.

The kiss went on and on until C.J. released her long enough to unfasten his jacket and place her arms around him. "Do you have any idea how much I want you? How long I've been starved for the feel of you?"

"Oh, yes," she said, searching his face in the semi-darkness, seeking for answers to the silent questions her heart was asking.

"I know we need to talk," he admitted. "And we will. Later." He fumbled for the zipper in the back of her dress and found none, then moved his fingers in search of the side closing. Adeptly he released the closure and loosened her silk gown.

With trembling fingers, she reached out and undid the buttons on his shirt. "Later," she whispered, and ran her hands across his broad, hairy chest, pushing his shirt farther apart. "You're such a beautiful man."

Bonnie Jean lowered her head and bestowed a series of moist kisses from one hard male nipple to the other.

C.J. ran his fingers through her hair and grasped her head in his big hands, forcing it upward. With his other hand, he lowered her dress until her unbound breasts fell free and the white silk draped her hips. "Heaven help us," he groaned. "I've only been half-alive without you."

He crushed her throbbing breasts into his chest, the feel so exquisite he thought he might explode from the contact of her bare flesh against his.

"You want me," she cried out. "You really want me."

"More than I've ever wanted anything in my life!" He wanted her desperately, with a hunger that bordered on madness.

He walked her backward toward a wicker chaise longue, and slowly, tenderly lowered her onto the plump cushions. She looked up at him and lifted her arms, issuing an invitation he couldn't refuse. He lowered his head to her breasts and took one pouting nipple into his mouth. Bonnie Jean groaned in tormented pleasure, running her fingernails across his muscular back.

All rational thought left her mind. She ceased to wonder why C.J. had finally succumbed to the passion raging between them. It didn't matter. Nothing mattered but the sweet agony of desire flowing through her.

"Kiss me again," she pleaded, threading her fingers through his hair, urging his head upward.

A sudden, glaring light filled the room, and through the haze of passion, Bonnie Jean heard a shrill female voice. "I think they're in here," Barbara Massey said. "Oh, dear. What's going on?"

C.J. lowered his body to cover Bonnie Jean's naked breasts. He turned slightly to look at Barbara and the two men, her brother Oliver and Whit Lowery, who were standing just inside the sun room doorway.

"Get the hell out of here," C.J. said.

"God, Carter," Whit said, his face scarlet. "I'm sorry. Barbara wanted us to help find you to make a toast to—"

"I said get out!" C.J. repeated.

Whit exited the room quickly, but Oliver and Barbara didn't move.

"I can't say I blame you," Oliver said. "But why here in your mother's house? You could have waited and taken her to a motel."

"Of course, if Bonnie Jean wasn't such a tramp, she would never have allowed this to happen." Barbara glared at Bonnie Jean, a look of envy and contempt in her eyes, then she turned and walked out, her brother following in her footsteps.

C.J. rose up and helped Bonnie Jean to her feet. "I'm sorry that happened."

She didn't say anything and she didn't look at him. She was utterly ashamed. Barbara Massey was right. This never would have happened if she'd acted like a lady instead of a two-bit tramp like her mother. God, what must C.J. think of her?

He grabbed her by the shoulders and tried to force her to look at him. "Bonnie Jean?"

She shook her head from side to side, but kept her eyes downcast, refusing to look at him. "Please let me go. Asking you for this date tonight was a big mistake."

She stepped away from him and rearranged her dress. Just as she had herself properly covered Dorothea Moody walked into the room, Wheeler Yancey a few steps behind her.

"I've just asked Barbara Massey and her brother to leave," Dorothea said, looking from her son to the disheveled woman at his side.

"You don't have to ask me to leave, Mrs. Moody," Bonnie Jean said. "I'll leave on my own if—" she looked at Wheeler "—if you'll let me borrow your car."

"You aren't going anywhere," C.J. said.

"Why don't you and Thea make sure Barbara and Oliver have left?" Wheeler told his nephew. "Give Bonnie Jean a few minutes to pull herself together."

"No." C.J. looked at Bonnie Jean and his heart broke at the hurt and shamed expression on her face. "All right, but I'll be back. Don't you dare go anywhere until we've talked."

As soon as C.J. and Dorothea left the room, Bonnie Jean fell into Wheeler's outstretched arms and buried her face in his black jacket, her body racked with sobs.

Then, quickly, she pulled herself together and held out her open palm.

"What?" he asked.

"Keys to the car."

"C.J. said not to leave until you two talk."

"Please, Wheeler. I can't stay. I'm sure Barbara told all those people out there what C.J. and I were doing."

"Loud and clear," Wheeler said. "I was so proud of Thea. She defended you. Said you and C.J. were engaged."

"Engaged? But…but that's not true."

Wheeler reached into his pocket, pulled out a set of keys and tossed them to Bonnie Jean "Go ahead and run, gal, if you think that'll solve anything."

"C.J. was treating me as if he really liked me. Now he'll hate me again. God, how could I have been so stupid?"

Wheeler chuckled. Leaning his big frame against the wall, he scratched his chin. "You two are like kerosene and a lit match. Put you together and there's bound to be an explosion."

"Please tell Dorothea how sorry I am." Bonnie Jean moved hurriedly past Wheeler and out of the sun room.

She retrieved her coat from the maid at the door and rushed outside, not stopping to reply to C.J.'s insistent yells. While running along the slippery sidewalk, she could hear C.J. calling her name, and when she slid inside Wheeler's black Corvette and inserted the key into the ignition, she saw C.J. coming toward her, motioning for her to stop. Ignoring him completely she started the car, revved the motor and backed out of the driveway, then turned onto the long, paved drive leading to the country road in front of the Yancey mansion.

Her body felt cold and damp from the frigid December night air and the freezing drizzle that coated her hair and clothes. Tears blurred her vision. She brushed them from her eyes and realized the car windshield had a thin layer of ice restricting her view.

Bright headlights glared through the back window and reflected off the rearview mirror. A car was following her, and the driver kept honking his horn. She knew it was C.J. Damn him! Why couldn't he just leave her alone?

Eight

Dammit, why wouldn't she stop? He'd done everything but run her off the road during the past fifteen minutes. He hoped she could see better than he could through the constant drizzle of frozen rain. If it got much worse, they'd both wind up in a ditch.

She exited off Highway 72 at the four-way stop, and he followed, thankful when she slowed down and turned into the parking lot between Cody's Poolroom and the all-night Laundromat. Undoubtedly she was having as difficult a time seeing the road as he was. He pulled his white Mercedes up beside Wheeler's Corvette, opened the door and stepped out into the frigid air and pelting sleet. He heard her car door slam and saw her make a mad dash for Cody's. When he called her name, her step faltered, but she kept moving and quickly disappeared inside the poolroom.

Bonnie Jean shut the door in his face. C.J. hesitated for a split second. The raw wind cut through his evening clothes, and the sleet began to soak into his skin. Grabbing the doorknob with chilled fingers, he opened the door and rushed into Cody's. Sweet warmth caressed his face and began spreading through his cold body. He looked over the poolroom quickly and found the place empty except for Cody, himself and Bonnie Jean, who'd seated herself at a table on the far side of the room.

He took several tentative steps in her direction, then stopped and watched her. She sat with her back to him, her shoulders slumped, her head bent. All he wanted to do was take her in his arms and comfort her, to tell her what a fool he'd been and beg her for that second chance his mother and uncle had been trying so hard to give them.

The sound of Roy Orbison's voice filled the room with heartbreaking tenderness and emotional intensity. "It's Over" seemed far too appropriate to C.J. as he turned toward the bar and saw Cody staring at him, curiosity evident in the big redhead's dark eyes.

"Evening, Carter," Cody said in his deep North Alabama drawl. "You and Bonnie Jean picked a fine night to stop by."

"You serving anything besides beer tonight?" C.J. asked, seating himself at the bar.

"Got some whiskey. My own personal stock," Cody said. "But it's not for sale." He reached under the bar and pulled out a bottle of Jack Daniel's, then set two glasses in front of C.J.

"I'd like a favor." C.J. leaned over the bar and

lowered his voice. "I need some time alone with Bonnie Jean."

Both C.J. and Cody glanced across the room at the woman huddled in a chair, her slender shoulders trembling. Cody poured the whiskey into the two glasses and nodded his head.

"I was just fixing to close for the night." Cody reached into his pocket and tossed C.J. a key ring. "Lock up for me."

"Thanks," C.J. said. "I owe you one."

Grabbing his sheepskin jacket off a nearby coat-rack, Cody headed for the front door. "Merry Christmas, you two," he said as he left.

Leaving the drinks on the bar, C.J. went to the front door and locked it. He slipped out of his wet evening jacket and threw it on top of the bar before picking up the two glasses of whiskey and walking across the room. "Only the Lonely" began playing on the radio seconds after the DJ announced that for two hours they would be paying tribute to the late, great Roy Orbison.

C.J. set one glass down in front of Bonnie Jean. She didn't look up or acknowledge his presence in any way. He took the chair beside her and set his drink down on the table.

"You should take off that wet coat," he said.

She clutched the coat more tightly around her.

"You're probably frozen to the bone." He pushed the glass closer to her. "Drink up. It's Cody's private stock."

She looked like a lost and frightened child sitting there hugging herself, her hair damp, her cheeks and nose pink from the cold. He knew that she was embarrassed and ashamed, and it was his fault. He shouldn't have tried to make love to her at his mother's house during the party. But he had wanted her so desperately, for such a long time, that he'd allowed his desire to take precedent over his common sense.

"Bonnie Jean, I'm sorry about what happened tonight."

She raised her head slightly and, with cautious eyes, looked at him. "Yeah, I know."

The pain in her voice squeezed his heart tightly. She was taking all the blame, and she had misunderstood why he regretted what had taken place in his mother's sun room. "I'm not sorry that we almost made love." He reached out for her, trying to take her hand. She scooted her chair away from him. "I'm sorry that I chose the wrong time and place. I'm sorry I put you in such an embarrassing position."

Bonnie Jean swiped the tears from her cheeks, trying to pretend they weren't there, trying to pretend she wasn't dying inside. "All I've ever been is an embarrassment to you. Eighteen years ago…and now."

He moved his chair closer to hers, and before she could stop him, he grabbed both of her hands. He felt her shaking, saw the tears in her eyes, and heard her labored breathing. "I have been the biggest fool on God's green earth. You were right when you said that I've been fighting myself."

With trembling fingers, Bonnie Jean raised her hand to her mouth in an effort to stop her teeth from chattering. C.J. squeezed her hand tightly. Tremors racked her body as she tried to summon her courage. "What's going on, C.J.? You've got me confused. Why this sudden change of heart?"

He held her hands in a death grip, afraid she'd pull away from him. "Before the party tonight, Mother told me something she should have told me years ago."

Bonnie Jean opened her eyes wide and stared directly at him. The quivering in her body increased. "What…what did she tell you?"

"The truth." C.J. stood, pulling Bonnie Jean to her feet. He held her small, cold hands within his tenacious grasp.

"About the…the ten thousand dollars?" she asked.

"Yes."

"You know I didn't ask for it, and I never got a dime of it?"

"Yes."

Bonnie Jean swayed backward. He caught her and dragged her shuddering body up against him. Damn, she's soaking wet and shaking like a leaf, he thought. "Come on, honey, let's get you out of this wet coat."

Obediently, like a docile child, she allowed him to remove her coat, but when he started to take her back into his arms, she resisted. "Did she tell you about Bubba?"

"She told me what she knew." He tried again to pull her back into his arms. She stepped away.

Like a haunting reminder of the years without Bonnie Jean, "In Dreams" began to play on the radio. How many lonely nights had he dreamed of her, only

to awaken alone and hurting? The dreams had seemed
so real—she had belonged to him and no one else—
her sweet lips, her laughing smile, her loving body,
her seductive voice. He had taken her with all the
passion and love they had once shared, but when he
awoke, she wasn't there. All that remained were the
memories and the repressed tears his masculinity refused to release.

"Why didn't you tell me what happened?" He
moved toward her, but stopped when she edged backward. "In the name of heaven, Bonnie Jean, why
didn't you make me understand? How could you have
let Mother and Sally destroy what we had together?"

"Even now, you don't understand, do you?" She
backed up to the wall, spread her open palms against
the smooth paneled surface, and took a deep breath,
trying to calm the raging emotions running rampant
within her.

"You've put us through hell for eighteen years!"
He hadn't realized how angry he was. Angry at Bonnie Jean.

"What about you?" she screamed, thrusting her
hands in front of her in a pleading gesture.

"You took away the only woman I ever loved, you
destroyed my life, you made me incapable of ever
loving again."

"What do you think you did to me? If we could
do it over again…" She moved away from the wall
and began walking around the room, her nervous
steps quickening when C.J. followed.

"But we can't. Nothing can change the past."

Bonnie Jean stood behind one of the pool tables,

her eyes damp with tears and her hands clutched tightly together against her breasts. "All I ever wanted was you. I loved you so much."

"And what about now?" he asked, moving toward her slowly, cautiously.

"What...what about now?"

"Do you still love me?"

Dear Lord, do I still love him? Did she still breathe? Did her heart still beat? "Do you... want...want a second chance?" She couldn't ask if he still loved her. She couldn't bear it if he said no.

"I want you. I've spent eighteen years wanting you, remembering what it was like between us."

"You remember the sex." She gripped the edge of the pool table with her trembling fingers.

"The hottest, wildest sex I've ever known." He stood on one side of the table watching her, passion controlling his body, desire glowing in his pale blue eyes.

"Don't come any closer," she warned, and picked up a cue ball from the neatly racked triangle.

C.J. laughed. "What are you afraid of, honey?"

"I...I want a second chance. A second chance for love."

"Sex is a part of love, isn't it?" He took a tentative step around the table.

"Stop!" When he kept walking toward her, she threw the cue ball at him. It hit him on the shoulder and bounced off.

"I want you, Bonnie Jean. Right here. Right now."

"No. Not like this." He took another step forward.

She picked up two more balls and threw them at him. One just missed his head and the other struck him squarely in the chest. "We need to talk."

"We'll talk." He continued moving around the table while she threw one ball after another at him in an attempt to stop his steady progress in her direction.

"We'll talk now." She threw the last ball, then backed up against the rack of cue sticks hanging on the wall. "There's so much I need to explain. So many things you still don't know."

"We can talk later. Right now, I want to rip that dress off you and run my hands all over your body."

"No, C.J."

"I want to kiss you until you can't breathe."

She reached up on the wall and removed a cue stick. "This isn't fair."

"I want to hold your breasts, I want to feel your nipples beneath my fingers. I want to take you in my mouth and caress you until you're crying with pleasure." His last step brought him to within a few feet of her.

Bonnie Jean pointed the cue stick at him. "Don't say those things."

"But they're what you want to hear, aren't they?" He felt the edge of the cue stick touch his chest. "Dammit, why are you fighting me when you want this as much as I do?"

"I want love, not just sex."

"Then teach me how to love again," he said, reaching out to take the cue stick away from her. He dropped the stick on the floor and pulled Bonnie Jean into his arms.

His last words were her undoing. *Then teach me how to love again.* He held her in his arms, and she knew this was where she belonged—where she had always belonged. She was C.J. Moody's woman, and nothing and no one could ever change that fact.

"I've never loved anyone else," she said, staring up at him with love and desire in her eyes.

He took the back of her head in one big hand, threading his fingers through the white-gold silk of her hair. "Good."

He didn't say what she longed to hear, that he'd never loved anyone else, that he loved her still. But she could wait for the words because his eyes and hands and body spoke a language she understood. Hunger rippled through her, so intense it was almost frightening, and she saw the same eager fury reflected in his eyes.

"No sweet words," he groaned, his lips against her neck. "No long, slow prelude. Only this!"

He took her mouth greedily. Hard and demanding, his kiss ravished her, seeking, conquering, wild with need. She responded with the same sizzling passion, giving back with the same urgency. She felt the hot shove of his tongue as it entered her mouth, and quivers of promised ecstasy racked her body. Their mouths and lips and tongues played out a rhapsody of torrid longing. Licking, nipping, sucking, plunging. Give and take. Warm and wet and sweet.

He bent his head to her chest, his lips covering the rounded swell of her breasts at the crisscrossed cleavage of her dress. "I want to see you." He put his hands at her waist and lifted her up onto the edge of the pool table. "I want my mouth on you."

Her legs hung over the side of the table. While he unzipped her white silk dress, she kicked off her shoes and let them drop to the floor. The soft thud of her heels hitting the wooden surface came a split second before the sound of Roy Orbison's "Pretty Woman" surrounding them. The wild, almost savage beat of drums and guitar stroked their senses, filling them with a stimulating rhythm to match the primeval pulse of their own sexuality.

With demanding hands, C.J. spread her legs apart and stepped between them, then with an impatient tug, her jerked her dress to her waist.

Her eyes softened with desire. Her mouth parted on an expectant sigh. Her whole body began to melt, slowly, ever so slowly, preparing for his possession.

He ran his hands down her neck, across her shoulders and over her breasts. She fell against him, moaning. Lifting her slightly, he lowered his head to one turgid nipple. When his lips encompassed her, she cried out. Pleasure so strong she thought she'd die surged through her.

"How did I live without you? Without this?" C.J. asked as he placed both of his big hands on her knees and began pushing her dress upward.

Inch by inch, the soft silk crept up her thighs until it rested about her hips. He looked at her. Hot need consumed him when he saw the sheer stockings and lacy garter belt. "Oh, baby."

With panting breath, she said, "I remember how much you always liked me in a garter belt."

"Show me you belong to me," he said, his voice a deep, sensuous roar in her ears. "Only to me." He stroked her naked back.

"I've never belonged to anyone else."

"Prove it to me," he whispered in her ear, then circled it with the moist heat from his open mouth.

Bonnie Jean gasped, clutching his shoulders as his tongue moved in a circular motion from the top of her ear to the lobe and back again.

He covered her neck with an untamed shower of kisses, and scorched her shoulders and back and breasts with the heat of his touch. He cupped her breasts in his hands, watching the way they filled his palms. Suddenly his mouth closed about her nipple.

She moaned, her whole body shivering from the delicious pleasure his hands and mouth created. She could no more resist this man than the earth could resist the pull of the moon.

C.J. raised his head, his eyes silvery pale. He fondled the underside of her breasts, then lifted their swollen weight. The pressure of his fingers increased, squeezing harder and harder until she groaned with tormented pleasure.

He moved his hands down her body, stopped at the top of her thighs, and slipped his fingers beneath one of the garter straps. He had never seen anything as beautiful as Bonnie Jean, half sitting, half lying before him, her body his for the taking. Her blond hair hung wild and free, her hazel eyes glowed with love, her large breasts heaved provocatively with each breath she took.

With remarkable speed, C.J. snapped loose each catch on her garter belt. ''I've dreamed of this.''

''So have I.'' She leaned back, spreading her arms behind her, placing her palms flat against the smooth felt top of the pool table.

''I'm aching. I need to be…inside you.'' He eased her stocking down her leg, tossed it aside and did the same with the other.

''I want you. I want it all.''

''Baby, I'll give you everything.'' He leaned over her, crushing her breasts against his hard chest.

Rising slightly, he spread her legs farther apart and lifted her just enough to remove her white lace bikini panties. A curiously exciting panic radiated through her. He stroked her breasts, rubbed his hand across her stomach and caressed her hips through the silk dress. Then with an aching urgency, he moved his hand lower and slipped inside to fondle the damp core of her femininity.

''C.J.,'' she whimpered, her feverish body bucking forward, her hips squirming against the table.

''Touch me.''

''Oh…'' She cried out, instinctively curling her legs about his thighs.

He pulled her hands to his chest. ''Unbutton my shirt.''

She quickly loosened the tiny buttons and spread back the crisp white material, easing it off his big shoulders and down his arms. Hesitantly she let her fingers curl around his hairy forearms, then glide upward to the bulge of muscles above his elbow.

"You make me crazy," she said. "You know that, don't you?"

He took her mouth with such masterful force that she clung to his shoulders while he grabbed her head, holding her to him. As their mouths burned into each other with a consuming blaze, their hands moved wildly over each other's bodies, stroking the red-hot flames within them to an uncontrollable white heat.

"I've wanted you day and night for eighteen years."

She reached out, running her fingertips over his cheek. "And I've wanted you."

"Every day I remembered the feel of you beneath me. Every night I dreamed of possessing you again and again, hearing you cry out my name."

She raked her fingers through the thick, dark hair covering his chest, her mouth moving with tormenting seduction down his neck and across his shoulders, her sharp, white teeth nibbling in hungry passion, leaving stinging, rosy nicks on his damp flesh.

"I love you." She lowered her hand to his belt, loosened it and slid down the zipper of his black trousers.

"Yes, baby…yes."

She eased her hand inside his dark briefs, finding the evidence of his arousal, closing about his hardness, feeding his hunger. "I want you. I want you inside me, now."

"Now?"

She tugged at his briefs, lowering them to reveal his naked beauty. "Don't make me wait."

He sighed against her breasts while he moved his

fingers in a stimulating gesture against her woman-hood. "You're hot and wet and ready."

With her arms and legs wrapped tightly around him, she accepted his touch as he lowered her down on the pool table, her body open for his possession. She arched her hips upward, invitingly.

For a few feverish moments, he tortured her nipples with his rough fingers, then ran his hands downward and across her stomach. Lowering himself to accommodate a swift, powerful joining, he grabbed her hips, positioning her, then thrust inside her welcoming body. They both cried out with pleasure. His over-whelming need drove him into her with repeated wild lunges, each move stimulating her more and more, drawing her closer to fulfillment.

"You feel so good, baby. Even better than I re-member." He moved his lips from breast to breast, sucking with an insatiable thirst.

"Oh, yes. Harder," she cried out, her nails mer-cilessly scraping his back, her body falling headlong into sweet, climactic oblivion.

She convulsed around him, tremors of release flow-ing from her body to his. His hot, sweaty flesh mated to hers as his lips murmured her name again and again. "You're mine, Bonnie Jean. Mine."

"Always," she said, her body sticking to his with the moisture of their shared perspiration.

With one final lunge, he took her once again to the apex of pleasure. They clung to each other, sharing in the culmination of a love so long denied.

C.J. stood, pulled his briefs and trousers up his legs, and adjusted them. His shirt hung open, revealing his broad, hairy chest. Bonnie Jean lay back on the table and watched him. Not even in her dreams had loving C.J. been like this. She smiled, that soft, satisfied smile of a woman who'd been thoroughly loved.

"Cody's got a cot in the back room." C.J. nodded to a half-open door. "He used to let me sleep it off in there when I had one too many. When I was a kid trying to act like a man."

"Are you asking me to stay here with you tonight?" She sat up on the edge of the table, but didn't bother to try to cover her nakedness. The silk gown lay bunched around her hips, wrinkled and damp.

"I want to make love to you all night. Slow and sweet. Hot and wild. I want to learn every inch of your body all over again."

She opened her arms to him. "I want that, too, but first, I have to tell you about…about Bubba."

She saw his whole body grow taut at the mention of her dead husband. There was still so much she had to explain to C.J.—about Bubba and their marriage. About Cara Jean.

"If we have to talk tonight, we'll talk." C.J. lifted Bonnie Jean off the pool table, swinging her up in his arms. She flung her arm around his neck and buried her face against his shoulder. He walked to the back of the poolroom, kicked open the door and moved inside the small, windowless storeroom. Light from the pool hall poured in, spreading a golden glow across the small cot resting against the wall.

C.J. set Bonnie Jean on her feet, then eased her dress down her body to her ankles. She stepped out of the white silk puddle and kicked the dress aside.

C.J. removed his shirt, his trousers, briefs, shoes and socks while she watched him undress. They stood before each other totally naked, a man and a woman.

Together they sat down on the cot. C.J. took her into his arms and guided her backward, his big body following. They lay down on the cot, side by side, her breasts flattened against his chest, his hairy legs rubbing against her smooth flesh, his hardening manhood throbbing against her belly.

C.J. reached down and pulled the single cotton blanket over them. Bonnie Jean snuggled into his warmth.

"I'm listening," he said.

She wasn't sure where to begin or how to explain. "You know that Bubba and I had been buddies since we were in diapers."

"Yeah."

"We'd never been anything more than friends." She laid her hand on C.J.'s chest.

"When did that change?" He hadn't realized he was holding his breath until he heard her reply.

"Not until after we married."

"Until then, I was the only one?" He pulled her tighter against him.

"What you saw that night when you came by the house was a setup." She took a deep, calming breath. "It was Mama and Bubba's plan. They knew it was the one sure way to break us up."

"Damn Sally Vickers." His fingers bit into the soft flesh on Bonnie Jean's hips. "And damn my mother, too."

"I never loved Bubba."

"Then why the hell did you marry him?"

She knew she should tell him about Cara Jean, but she was afraid. What if she told him and he couldn't forgive her? She wanted tonight, just tonight. She'd tell him, she promised herself, but later, when they'd had a chance to rebuild some of what they'd lost.

"Things were over between us," she said. "You had left the country. Bubba needed somebody to take care of Elaine. So…so I just married him."

C.J. looked at her. She wasn't telling him the whole truth, he realized. She was holding something back. "Have we talked enough for tonight?" he asked.

"What?" She noticed the sexy smile on his lips and breathed a sigh of relief that he hadn't asked any more questions.

"I don't want to think about the past. I want to concentrate on the present. On you and me, and the pleasure we can give each other." Whatever secrets she was keeping from him, he'd discover tomorrow or the next day or the next. He'd spent a lifetime without this woman. He didn't intend to spend another night without her.

"Is this our second chance?" she asked. "After all this time, have we finally hit it lucky?"

"After all this time, lady, I've come to my senses. I don't know if I can learn to love again. I've spent eighteen years building up a wall of hate inside me."

"Oh, C.J., I did that to you, didn't I?"

"If anyone can undo it, Bonnie Jean, you can."

"I'm going to try. I'm going to try damn hard."

Nine

Bonnie Jean tried to move, but she was trapped beneath the weight of a large, hairy arm. Opening her eyes slowly, she stared up at the mildewed ceiling of Cody's storeroom, then turned her head to look at the big man sleeping soundly beside her on the small cot. She lay on her back, he on his side. The warmth of his naked body snuggled against hers stirred anew the desire she'd felt for endless hours during the night and early morning.

She couldn't take her eyes off C.J. She had dreamed of this—awakening in his arms after a night of ecstasy. A few times, she'd almost given up hope of ever again sharing the joys of loving she could find only with this special man.

He looked so peaceful lying there, a day's growth of beard darkening his face. The blanket had slipped below his waist, leaving his chest and stomach un-covered. Bonnie Jean could see clearly the scar mar-ring the perfection of C.J.'s abdomen. With hesitant fingers, she reached out and touched the puckered flesh. When he took a deep breath, she jerked her hand away and checked to see if she had awakened him.

His eyes were still closed and he hadn't moved, so, assuming he was sleeping, Bonnie Jean continued staring at him, savoring the precious sight of the man she loved.

Then without warning, she found herself jerked up off the bed and over on top of her lover. Her naked body tingled with excitement everywhere it touched his.

"Good morning," he said, smiling up at her. "Beautiful morning, isn't it?"

She laughed, lowered her head and gave him a quick kiss on his open lips. "How do you know it's a beautiful morning? There are no windows in this room."

"Hell, woman, I don't care if there's ten feet of snow outside, it's a beautiful morning in here, in this bed." He moved his hands from her waist, running them down her hips. Grasping the rounded firmness of her buttocks, C.J. pressed her body more intimately into his own. "And things are getting better by the minute."

"I just want to know one thing," she said, placing her hands on each side of his head in order to brace her body when she raised herself above him. "How on earth can an old man of forty have such stamina?"

Amusement sparkled in her eyes and curled her love-swollen lips into a smile.

Laughter rumbled deep in his chest. "An old man, huh?" He surged upward, the undeniable hardness of his body seeking the soft sanctuary of hers. "I'll show you an old man."

"Show me, show me," she teased, opening herself for his possession.

Holding her hips, he positioned her atop him and surged into her body with all the urgency he'd been unable to fully sate in the previous hours. It had always been this way with Bonnie Jean. Wild, hot and almost unbearable in its intensity. And never enough, no matter how many times he took her.

His lips sought and found her breasts. In a frenzy of loving, he moved from one tightly pouting nipple to the other, eliciting a cry of pleasure from Bonnie Jean.

Her body quickly picked up his rhythm and she began to teach his a new cadence. Slower, deeper, harder. He suckled at her breast while he caressed the sides of her hips and thighs, petting her, fondling her softness until he was so tight and hard within her that he wasn't sure how much longer he could hold back.

The tempo of her ride quickened to a frantic pace as layer after layer of pleasure built inside her. "Faster, faster," she moaned, throwing her head back and licking her own lips with the sheer sensuality that coursed through her.

"Faster." He bucked upward, lifting his big body into her smaller one. "Deeper. All the way."

With one final, vigorous lunge, he brought her to

completion and joined her in a mutual release that left them both replete and exhausted.

She lay on top of him, her head resting on his damp flesh. The curly hairs on his chest tickled her nose, and she buried her face against him. He soothed her with gentle hands and said a silent prayer to a most benevolent God that He'd seen fit to bring Bonnie Jean back into his life and give them a second chance.

Neither of them moved for a long, sweet time, and not one word was exchanged to break the magic afterglow. C.J. eased Bonnie Jean onto the cot beside him and kissed her playfully on the nose.

"I'm starving," he said. "I'm so hungry I could eat a horse."

"I don't think Cody keeps any horse meat around here, but I know he's got a coffee maker. I've seen it." Bonnie Jean got up, glanced down at her naked body, and then looked around the room.

"You lose something?"

"My clothes." She laughed.

C.J. got up, his big body completely nude. "Yeah, I seemed to have lost mine somewhere along the way, too." After reaching down to retrieve his crumpled shirt from the floor, he tossed it to Bonnie Jean. "Put this on until after we've had coffee. Once we're completely awake and alert, I'll drive you home and you can feed me."

She caught the shirt and slipped into it, buttoning all but the top three buttons. The sleeves hung way beyond her hands and when she stood, the shirt touched the tops of her thighs halfway to her knees.

"Shouldn't you call home and let Dorothea and Wheeler know you're still alive?"

C.J. found his trousers, picked them up and tried to shake out a few of the wrinkles. He stepped into them and closed the zipper. "I'll call and tell them that you and I will be there for Christmas dinner this evening."

"Oh, C.J., are you sure? I mean—"

"Believe me, Mother will be delighted." He pulled Bonnie Jean into his arms and kissed her lightly on the lips. "She'll see it as a sign that we've forgiven her."

"I forgave her a long time ago," Bonnie Jean said, taking C.J.'s face in her hands. "She didn't know she would almost destroy our lives. She did what she did because she loves you."

"You're being very generous." He looked down at her and thought his heart would burst. It had been so long since he'd been able to experience so many emotions—to feel with such intensity. "But you're right. I can't hate my own mother for doing what she thought was right. Nothing can change what happened. Nothing can bring back what we lost."

She released her hold on his face, took his hand into hers and led him out into the poolroom. "Coffee. I need coffee." Bonnie Jean didn't want to think about the past, about all the wasted years. She didn't want to remember that she hadn't told him about the most precious thing they'd lost.

He swatted her naked behind and followed her to the bar. "We Wish You a Merry Christmas" was playing on the radio that they had forgotten to turn off the previous night. Seating himself, C.J. watched while she prepared a pot of coffee.

The windows had fogged up so much during the night that only a small amount of pane was left clear enough to see outside. C.J. held a dark red Alabama mug in his hand as he walked closer to the front window. "No sunshine," he said. "But it isn't sleeting or snowing, and the road doesn't look too bad."

Returning to the bar, he held out his cup while Bonnie Jean poured the steaming black coffee. She sipped the hot liquid in her orange Auburn mug. Now would be the perfect time to talk, she thought. They were alone, and she was reasonably sure they wouldn't be making love for a while. Seating herself beside him at the bar, Bonnie Jean placed her coffee mug on the counter and turned to C.J.

"What did last night and this morning mean to you?" she asked. "Where do we go from here?"

He eyed her over the rim of his mug as he tilted it to his lips. Well, he told himself, she has every right to know how you feel and what you think. The problem was he wasn't completely sure himself. The only thing he was certain of was his desire for Bonnie Jean. He wanted her sexually, and he wanted, more than anything, to be able to love her again. But was his heart capable of loving? Had he allowed himself to be consumed by hatred and jealousy and loneliness for so long that he was incapable of loving?

"Making love with you is the best thing that's happened to me in eighteen years," he said truthfully. "I want you just as much now as I ever did."

"I know." She clasped her hands together and be-

gan rubbing one hand with the other, her thumb stroking nervously across the inside of her fingers. "It's
the same with me."

"We both know we can't change what happened.
We can't erase the past eighteen years."

"But we can change the present and the future."

"I...I want us to have that second chance." He
hesitated briefly before continuing because he was
afraid of hurting her, and somehow he knew Bonnie
Jean had suffered enough. "I'm a hard man. Sometimes a cold and uncaring man."

"C.J.—"

When she protested, he placed one big finger on
her lips. "Shhh... I love Mother and Uncle Wheeler,
and I loved you once. But I've never loved anyone
else."

"Your wife?"

"There was no love between Kathie Lou and me.
There was respect and fondness, but no love."

"Then why..." Bonnie Jean felt a mixture of sad-
ness and relief. She'd braced herself to hear all about
how much C.J. had loved his wife and how perfect
their marriage had been. Selfishly she was glad that
he'd never loved another woman, but the thought of
C.J. enduring a loveless marriage brought tears to her
eyes.

With gentle fingers he wiped the tears from her
cheeks, then kissed her forehead. "Don't cry for me,
honey. I went into that marriage with my eyes wide
open. So did Kathie Lou. It was a case of money and
old family name marrying its own kind. And...we
both wanted a child."

Instant cold. Shivering dread. Bonnie Jean's body reacted to the mention of a child. C.J.'s child. When she told him the truth about Cara Jean, would he ever be able to forgive her? Or would he blame her the way she had always blamed herself? She couldn't bring herself to look at him. What if he could see her dark secret in her eyes?

"Of course, we didn't know at the time that Kathie Lou couldn't have children." It had been during his marriage to Kathie Lou that Barbara Massey had told him about Bonnie Jean and Bubba's child. He had never known such pain. For days afterward, he'd been half out of his mind picturing Bonnie Jean with Bubba, a fat, healthy baby nursing at Bonnie Jean's breast. The child should have been his, dammit. The child should have been his. It wasn't until Bonnie Jean returned to Tuscumbia after Bubba's motorcycle accident that he'd found out the child had died years ago.

"I'm sorry," she said, and meant it. C.J. should have a child to carry on the Yancey-Moody line. What would the world be like without a little Carter Jackson Moody V? she wondered.

"I heard that you had a child." He realized the memories were painful, but they needed to talk about all of it—all the years they'd been apart.

"Yes." *I can't tell him now. Please Lord, give me just a little more time.*

"It must have been terrible for you and Bubba when you lost her." C.J. reached out to put his arm around Bonnie Jean, but she pulled away and stood up.

"I can't talk about our…my daughter. Not now. Later." She began pacing around the room. "Later, I'll tell you everything."

C.J. followed her to the front windows where she stood gazing out at their cars in the parking lot. "Did you and Bubba have a good marriage?" He put his arms around her and drew her into his embrace.

She snuggled against him and laid her head on his chest. "My marriage to Bubba was a nightmare. We were friends who should have remained just that."

"Why the hell did you run off to Nashville and marry him?"

"At the time, I thought it was the best thing to do." She couldn't tell him that she had just found out she was pregnant and would have made a bargain with the devil in order to keep her child. "I practically raised Elaine. She was only ten when we married."

"What went wrong?" C.J. asked, hating himself for being glad that she and Bubba hadn't been deliriously happy.

"Bubba knew I loved you, and that…well, that affected our relationship." Somehow she couldn't bring herself to tell C.J. that every time Bubba touched her she cringed, and the only way she had endured the sexual side of their marriage was by pretending that the man invading her body was the man she loved.

"Yeah, I understand. Kathie Lou knew about you."

"How? Who would have been cruel enough to tell her?"

"I did."

"What?"

"The first time I made love to her, I called out your name."

Complete silence filled Cody's poolroom. C.J. and Bonnie Jean stood holding each other, comforting each other, trying desperately to soothe the pain from a past neither of them could change.

C.J. escorted Bonnie Jean from the dining room into the parlor and seated her on the rose-colored Victorian sofa in front of the fireplace. Cedar logs burned brightly, miniature white lights adorning the eight-foot Christmas tree blinked on and off, and the aroma of evergreen permeated the elegant room.

"Would anyone care for something to drink before we open our presents?" Dorothea asked, seating herself in a moss green velvet chair beside the sofa.

"I'll open up a bottle of bubbly later, Thea," Wheeler said, moving to stand directly behind his sister's chair. "Let's see what goodies old Saint Nick brought us."

C.J. smiled at Bonnie Jean and winked, then knelt down in front of the enormous tree. "I guess we'll see who's been naughty and who's been nice."

Dorothea Moody laughed, and when Bonnie Jean looked at her and smiled, Dorothea smiled back and reached across the few inches that separated them to pat Bonnie Jean on the hand. "I haven't seen him like this in years," she whispered. "Thank you, my dear."

"Here you go, Uncle Wheeler." C.J. handed his uncle the present he'd purchased—an antique pistol to add to his already-extensive collection. "And this one's for you, Mother." He gave her the sapphire-and-diamond earrings he'd chosen especially for her.

C.J. distributed the gaily wrapped Christmas gifts one by one until there were only three presents under the tree. Since they were all small items, he lifted all three and placed them in Bonnie Jean's lap, then sat down beside her.

"Open Mother's and Uncle Wheeler's first," he told her, arranging the gifts in precise order where they lay on her thighs. "Save mine for last."

"These are for me?" Bonnie Jean knew she was going to cry, and couldn't stop herself. "But…but I don't have anything for you…or your mother. And… and I left Wheeler's gift at the house."

"It's all right, Bonnie Jean," Dorothea said. "You can give me two gifts next year."

"I…I don't know what to say."

"Open them." Wheeler placed his big hands on his sister's shoulders and gave her a loving squeeze. "And then you can say thank you."

She opened the gift from Wheeler first. It was a music box that played Debussy's "Clair de lune."

"Oh, Wheeler, it's simply beautiful. Thank you."

"You're welcome, gal. Thought you'd like it."

With nervous fingers, she opened Dorothea's gift, all wrapped in silver paper and white ribbon. She couldn't imagine C.J.'s mother giving her a present. The box was tiny, and the contents lay hidden beneath a protective layer of tissue. Bonnie Jean reached inside and withdrew a thimble.

"It's an enamel thimble. Blue Willow." Dorothea's voice quivered.

Bonnie Jean looked at the older woman and saw the apprehension in her pale blue eyes. Suddenly she realized how important it was to C.J.'s mother that she like the gift. "It's lovely, Mrs. Mo...Dorothea."

With just a touch of anxiety left in her voice, Dorothea said, "It's from my own collection. One of my favorites. I...I thought, perhaps we could start you a collection." She looked at Bonnie Jean, obviously seeking approval. "That is...if you'd like."

Bonnie Jean's eyes clouded with tears—tears of happiness. "I think that's a wonderful idea. But, of course, you'd have to tell me how to go about it, where to buy them and all that."

"Oh, my dear, I'd be delighted." Dorothea smiled and wiped the tears from her misty eyes.

C.J. picked the final gift up from Bonnie Jean's lap and handed it to her. "One more, and then Wheeler and I will go get that chilled bottle of champagne. I think we've all got something to celebrate this year."

"Hear. Hear." Wheeler's deep voice boomed.

The box in her hand was quite small, rectangular in shape and rather thin. She couldn't imagine what was inside, or when C.J. had found the time to buy it. She opened the gift, which was encased in a plastic container. A note was attached. Bonnie Jean read the words written in C.J.'s big, bold script. *No more bad memories. No more hatred and pain. The future will be what we make it. Teach me to love again.*

Bonnie Jean froze, her entire body became rigid as she looked beneath the note. When she saw the tape, she threw herself into C.J.'s arms and hugged him fiercely. "I will. I promise," she whispered just before she kissed him.

"What on earth is it?" Dorothea asked. "It looks like some sort of cassette tape."

In Bonnie Jean's exuberance, she'd dropped the tape. Wheeler walked around Dorothea's chair, picked up the gift and inspected it. "It's a Patsy Cline tape."

"Oh," Dorothea said.

Bonnie Jean reached out and took the tape from Wheeler, her eyes moist and bright, her face aglow with happiness. "It's the best present—the best."

C.J. laughed when he saw the puzzled look on his mother's face and the quizzical glint in Wheeler's eyes. "Champagne time, Uncle Wheeler."

"You two gals hold the fort down and we'll be right back," Wheeler said.

After Wheeler and C.J. left the room, Dorothea Moody turned to Bonnie Jean. "I want to thank you for being so kind to me, my dear. I know I don't deserve it."

"C.J. and I have agreed that it won't change the past to blame anyone for what happened. We…we all did what we thought was best at the time." Bonnie Jean reached out and took Dorothea's hand. "You can't know what it means to me that you're willing to accept me as a part of C.J.'s life."

"If only I'd been that wise eighteen years ago."

"It wasn't your fault. If I had been more mature, less insecure…"

"I haven't seen Carter act so carefree in years. You can make him happy."

"I'm going to try."

Dorothea held Bonnie Jean's hand tightly. "Have the two of you worked out everything? I mean…have you been totally honest with each other about… Kathie Lou and Bubba and—"

"We've discussed our feelings. In the past and the present. I know what a farce C.J.'s marriage was, and he knows what a nightmare mine was."

"Have you told him about the child?" Dorothea grabbed both of Bonnie Jean's hands and squeezed forcefully.

"No. I wanted to give us a little time…just a few days. I'm so afraid…so afraid."

Dorothea moved onto the sofa beside Bonnie Jean and took the younger woman into her arms, patting her soothingly on the back. "You must tell him. He'll understand."

"Will he? Can he ever forgive me, when I've never been able to forgive myself?"

"Oh, my dear, what happened wasn't your fault. You were all alone with no one to turn to for help. If only I'd—don't you think I have my share of guilt? If I hadn't turned away from you, refused to give you C.J.'s address overseas, you would never have married Bubba Harland and moved off to Nashville. If only I had accepted you and your baby…"

"Champagne, ladies," Wheeler announced as he walked into the parlor and popped the cork on an aged bottle.

Wheeler poured and C.J. passed out the glasses. Everyone stood when C.J. proposed a toast. "To a new year and a new life."

* * *

C.J. and Bonnie Jean sat alone in the parlor. The glowing embers of the fire lighted the room with golden animated shadows. An empty bottle of champagne stood upside down inside the silver ice bucket atop the piano.

Bonnie Jean ran her bare foot up and down over C.J.'s. She cuddled closer to him. He shifted his weight on the delicate Victorian sofa and pulled Bonnie Jean onto his lap.

Dreams really do come true, she thought. She couldn't ever remember being this happy. But, she had learned that happiness was an ephemeral thing— as elusive as unicorns and mermaids and knights in shining armor, and perhaps, just as fanciful.

"You and Mother seemed awfully chummy when Uncle Wheeler and I came in with the champagne," he said.

"Dorothea and I are going to be friends." Bonnie Jean took his hand in hers and brought it to her lips.

"I see." He outlined her lips with his fingertips.

"You're going to have to take me home soon. It's after midnight."

"You could stay here and sleep in my bed." He took her face in his hands, caressing her cheeks with his thumbs.

"You know I can't do that." She leaned over and rubbed his nose with her own. "I wouldn't be that disrespectful to your mother."

"Then I'll spend the night with you at your house." His lips covered hers with a quick and tempting kiss.

"Everyone in Tuscumbia will know by noon to-morrow."

"My dear Ms. Harland, don't you realize that the whole county is probably already talking about the fact that you and I spent the entire night locked up inside Cody's poolroom?"

"Oh, my goodness!" Bonnie Jean gasped and pulled out of C.J.'s arms. "I didn't even think about that. Oh, no. Your mother will be so upset. And you, oh C.J., you must hate the idea that we're the subject of town gossip again."

Pulling her back into his arms, C.J. silenced her worried chatter with another kiss, a kiss that added assurance to what he said afterward. "You may find this hard to believe, but I don't give a damn what people are saying." He laughed, loud and hard and long. The kind of laughter that came from a man's soul—free and unrestrained.

"But...but as long as we continue our affair, we're going to be the talk of Tuscumbia. Can you honestly say that it won't bother you when Oliver Merritt and his kind make snide remarks about us?"

"If Oliver Merritt or any other man says one thing about us, he's liable to find his teeth shoved down his throat."

"Are you aware that you aren't thinking or talking much like a Southern gentleman?"

"You're right," he said, slipping his hand underneath her black wool skirt. "To maintain my image, I suppose I'd have to challenge Oliver to a duel."

"C.J.!" She squealed when he moved his hand up her thigh and slid his fingers inside her silky panties.

"Nothing is going to come between us this time—nothing and no one. Not the past. Not all the pain. Not my mother or anyone else."

"There is still so much standing between us," she said, holding on to him as if she were afraid he might disappear at any moment. "We're going to have to work hard to make things right."

"There are no guarantees in this life. But we have a chance now, Bonnie Jean."

"Yes, my darling, we do."

The kiss was long and passionate and led to longer and more passionate ones. Finally they bundled up, left the Yancey mansion and drove to Sugar Hill. There in Sally Vickers's house, Bonnie Jean and C.J. made love until dawn. Not once did they think about tomorrow.

Ten

Sugar Hill pulsed with life as only a restaurant can on New Year's Eve. Completely booked and turning people away, *the* place to eat in the Shoals boasted a grand opening the likes of which few locals had ever seen. Soft, bluesy jazz saturated the classy Victorian house from the dance floor where the combo played to the upper level and basement where the live music was piped in. Formally attired waiters and waitresses swarmed like a host of drone bees, and haute cuisine was served alongside the standard T-bones and baked potatoes. Carts of fancy desserts tempted even the most finicky eater, and champagne corks popped with regularity.

Carter Jackson Moody IV stood in the foyer beside the fireplace. The Crane clock Bonnie Jean had purchased at the charity auction ticked away the minutes from its royal perch on the oak mantel. C.J. smiled and nodded at Polly Drew and Harvey Grimes as they passed by. Well, he thought, Bonnie Jean and Uncle Wheeler were right about this place. It's going to be a success and make some big profits for Yancey-Moody Enterprises. But then, his uncle was a shrewd businessman, and he'd discovered that Bonnie Jean knew the restaurant business inside out.

An austere young maître d' escorted newly arrived guests to their tables, and Bonnie Jean Harland, who'd been mixing and mingling with the clientele, sauntered in C.J.'s direction.

Smiling, he watched her come toward him. It took every ounce of his willpower to control his body's masculine urges. Not only was she beautiful tonight, but she was classy and sexy and tempting. And best of all, she was his. It felt so good to know that when this place closed tonight and the new year dawned, she'd be in his arms.

During the past week, they'd spent every night together, sharing the pleasures they'd so long denied themselves. They had mutually agreed not to discuss the past, to simply live for the present, one day at a time. But both of them realized that this temporary paradise couldn't last forever—they couldn't go on pretending the past didn't exist.

He could not take his eyes off her as she moved slowly, seductively across the foyer. Her shapely curves filled out the strapless green velvet gown she wore. Tiny diamond-and-emerald studs sparkled in her ears and a matching necklace draped her throat. They were his "Opening Night" gift to her, and he'd had the devil's own time persuading her to accept them.

Her pale hair was draped atop her head, and tiny curls circled her beautiful face. With each step her hips swayed in a naturally sensual gesture, and her bare shoulders shifted seductively. With each breath she took, her breasts moved enticingly, and her soft, red lips issued an unspoken invitation.

The cool, crisp sound of a piano blended with the hot, throaty moan of a saxophone. C.J. held out his hand. Bonnie Jean looked at him, all the love in her heart reflected in her eyes. She took his hand and allowed him to lead her into the main salon, past table after table of celebrators, and onto the dance floor.

He slipped his arm around her waist, his big hand resting on her hip. He took her hand in his, brought it to his lips and kissed it tenderly. "You are... breathtaking."

"You don't look so bad yourself." She ran her eyes over him in a quick, complimentary appraisal. Oh, yes, she thought. You look mighty good to me, Mr. Moody.

His dark evening clothes fit him with the smooth perfection only tailor-made attire could. His white shirt boasted a small row of ruffles down the front and at the cuffs. On a less masculine man, the effect might have been effeminate, but it simply added to the powerful aura of a man as big and overwhelmingly male as C.J. Moody.

He held her with possessive tenderness, their bodies so close they could feel each other's heartbeat. Although the dance floor was crowded, it disappeared from their view. He saw nothing except Bonnie Jean, the woman he desired above all others—the woman with whom he was beginning to fall in love all over again. She saw nothing except C.J., the man who owned her, body and soul—the only man she had ever loved.

She gazed up at him adoringly. He was, without a doubt, the most handsome man she'd ever seen. Tall and big. Broad-shouldered and muscular. Tanned and incredibly rugged for a man so beautiful. Moving her hand up his back, she caressed him with honest desire. She threaded her fingers through his hair where it touched his neck, longing to pull his head down to meet hers, yearning for the feel of his lips on hers.

Rising on tiptoe, she whispered in his ear as he guided her slowly around the dance floor. "I reserved one of the private rooms upstairs for us."

"Then what are we waiting for?" He slowed his pace, then stopped abruptly.

"Not now," she laughed. "I can't leave until we close Sugar Hill for the night. The room is for our own private New Year's celebration, later."

"I don't know if I can wait to…celebrate."

"We promised to welcome in the new year with Dorothea and Wheeler," she reminded him, and nodded toward the table where his relatives sat.

"So we did."

They continued dancing, their bodies taking pleasure in the intimate contact, yet craving more—much more. One dance ended and another began, but before the second dance ended, the band struck up a countdown beat and the crowd readied itself for the grand welcoming of January first.

Five…four…three…two…one…*Happy New Year!* The crowd went wild. Balloons fell from the ceiling by the hundreds, confetti scattered like dry leaves on a windy day, and party horns blasted while shouts of jubilation rang out loud and clear. The band began to play "Auld Lang Syne," and couples shared their first kiss of the new year.

C.J. and Bonnie Jean exchanged a long and searching look, each remembering how many New Years they had spent apart and both thankful that, at long last, they were together again. Instinctively she tilted her head as he lowered his. Their lips joined in a languid, half-hesitant kiss as if they were afraid to test the limits of their willpower with a more vital touch. But once their lips mated, it was too late to stop the tidal wave of desire that surged through each of them.

Without hesitation she opened her mouth, seeking the fury of his tongue, her own a willing participant in the soul-hungry kiss. He slid his big hands down her back and caught her hips, kneading tenderly before pulling her against him. She could feel him throbbing, and her own body quivered with response.

"If we're going to join Mother and Wheeler, now would be the perfect time…before I take you right here on the dance floor." C.J. held her hips tightly, rubbing her against him.

Quickly he released her and led her to Wheeler Yancey's table. Teenie Jeffreys sat beside Wheeler, her head resting on his shoulder. Dorothea Moody smiled at Bonnie Jean when she sat down beside her. C.J. seated himself across the table.

"Well, gal, this place is a hit," Wheeler said. "Looks like you and C.J. have got some restaurant here."

"I think so, too," Bonnie Jean said, reaching out to pat Wheeler's big, weathered hand where it clasped a glass of champagne sitting on the table. "And since Sugar Hill will be taking up all my time from now on, I plan to give The Plantation to Elaine for a wedding gift when she and Nick marry."

"How very generous of you, my dear." Dorothea's blue eyes widened in surprise as she stared at Bonnie Jean. "She's almost like a daughter to you, isn't she?"

"Yes." Bonnie Jean loved Elaine dearly. She had been the one good thing in her marriage to Bubba, the only thing that had helped her keep her sanity after Cara Jean's death.

"You'll have your hands full here." Wheeler lifted the champagne bottle and poured two glasses, then handed them to C.J. and Bonnie Jean. "Let's toast this bright new year."

"Oh, let's all make a toast, honey," Teenie Jeffreys said, snuggling closer to Wheeler. "And ladies first."

"Start us off, sweetie," Wheeler said.

Raising her glass, Teenie made her toast. "To family, friends and lovers."

Dorothea gasped quietly, Wheeler laughed heartily, and C.J. and Bonnie Jean exchanged knowing smiles.

"Mother?" C.J. asked.

"To new beginnings," Dorothea said, and looked directly at Bonnie Jean.

Bonnie Jean didn't hesitate when it came her turn. "To learning how to love again." Although they weren't touching, she could feel C.J. as surely as if she'd been in his arms.

"To a new generation of Yancey-Moodys, if God sees fit to bless us with them." Wheeler downed half a glass of bubbly in one gulp, then wiped his mouth with the back of his hand.

Bonnie Jean couldn't bring herself to look at C.J. Instead she glanced at Dorothea and saw tears in her eyes.

C.J. stood to give his toast. Everyone at the table looked up at him. "To Bonnie Jean."

She felt the tears lodge in her throat, threatening to choke her. Her body trembled slightly. It's too good to be true, she told herself. This can't last. When I'm completely honest with C.J., all this will come to an end. And she had to tell him soon because she knew he was already beginning to trust her—perhaps, already beginning to fall in love again.

C.J. held Bonnie Jean in front of him, draping his arms about her waist and holding her back against his chest. The first tentative light of dawn warmed the sky like candlelight spreading slowly across the horizon. The French windows in the upstairs private room at Sugar Hill were coated with a thin layer of frost, and the limbs of a nearby willow tree swayed back and forth to the rhythm of the wintry breeze. A hushed stillness surrounded the couple, the only sound coming from the crackling logs in the fireplace.

C.J. nuzzled her neck, then caressed the side of her face with his lips. "I don't think we'll ever rent this room. We should keep it just for us."

Bonnie Jean moved her head slightly from side to side, inspecting the romantic ambience she had created in this private dining room. The decor was Queen Anne. From the damask wing chairs to the cherry table graced with a white linen tablecloth and napkins, from the Haviland china to the Rogers silver and Waterford crystal. Candles glowed with elegant serenity from silver holders, their flickering light reflected in the intricately carved gilt mirror on the wall above the sofa.

"This room will be reserved for lovers only. For special occasions calling for a romantic background." Bonnie Jean turned in his arms, facing him, her eyes alight with love and desire. "I can't remember ever being this happy."

"It's been such a long time." He ran his big hands down her back and over her hips. Clutching her through the velvety softness of her evening gown, C.J. pulled her closer, the hardness of his body telling her of his need. "Being with you again, learning to let go of the past has given me back a part of myself I thought I'd lost forever."

Desperation chilled her. At the thought of losing C.J. again, Bonnie Jean clung to him, her slender fingers grasping, her lips seeking his for the reassurance her heart so badly needed. *Just this one last time,* she bargained with fate. *Give me this moment, this pre-*

cious moment, and I'll tell him the truth about Cara Jean.

"No matter what happens, never forget that I love you, that I've always loved you." She stood on tiptoe and slipped her arms around his neck, bringing his head down to meet hers.

"Honey, you act as if something terrible is going to happen." He kissed the tip of her nose. "The worst is all behind us. Only good times lie ahead."

"Oh, C.J., promise me. Promise me you'll remember I love you."

"Honey, what's the matter?"

"Nothing," she sighed, moving her lips up his neck and running her tongue across his jawline. "Promise me. Please."

"I promise." He covered her mouth with his, sealing the promise with a consuming passion. He wished he could soothe her fears, but not knowing what demon haunted her, he was helpless to assuage her uncertainties. "Can't you tell me what's bothering you?"

"It's nothing," she lied. "I'm being foolish. Forgive me."

"Are you afraid this—" he clasped her to him tightly, allowing her to feel his aching need against her "—and this—" he kissed her with tender abandon "—and this—" he looked into her eyes, conveying the depth of his emotions "—won't last? Are you afraid it's too good to be true?"

She couldn't help smiling. She reached out and touched his face with a steady hand. "I couldn't bear to lose you again. My life would be meaningless."

"Let's not borrow trouble, Bonnie Jean. Let's take each day as it comes. We've come so far in the last week. Now we have all the time in the world."

If only that were true, she thought. If only she didn't carry a dark and guilty secret in her heart, she could face the days ahead unafraid. But she couldn't let things progress any further between them without telling him the truth about his daughter. "We have today. We're alone in a room I designed for romance, and I want to share it with you. I want the memory of this one perfect morning."

He traced the outline of her lips with his fingertip. "Then let's do it right. We need more champagne. And music."

She whirled out of his embrace and across the room to the cherry Queen Anne secretary by the window. Opening the glass door to the top shelves, Bonnie Jean reached inside to where a CD player was placed. She inserted a disc and punched the Play button. The captivatingly delicate strains of Beethoven's *Moonlight Sonata* permeated the room. Eloquent in its simplicity, the haunting melody produced a dreamily romantic atmosphere, each precise and inspired piano note touching the heart of its listeners.

"Music," she said, then sauntered over to the silver bucket containing a chilled bottle of Dom Pérignon. "And champagne."

"Lady, you think of everything." He watched her uncork the bottle and pour the bubbling liquid into two glasses. When she lifted a glass out to him, he walked over to her and took the offering.

"To us," she said, and sipped the exquisite sparkling wine.

"To us." He saluted her with his glass and tilted it to his lips.

Bonnie Jean set her glass on the table. Her gaze locked with his. "I want to make love to you, C.J. Will you let me?"

"Will I..." Erotic images flickered through his mind, thoughts so wanton, he caught his breath on an aching groan.

She moved toward him with delicate slowness, each step a seductive gesture. Standing before him, she reached out and ran her fingertips over his face, his ears, his neck. "I want to undress you. I want to love you."

"And I want to love you." When he reached for her, she stepped backward. "Bonnie Jean?"

"You can love me later. Right now, you must let me give to you. Please. Allow me to pleasure you." She moved her hands across his shoulders, easing his tuxedo jacket off. She dropped the garment to the floor as she began unbuttoning his ruffled shirt.

When all the buttons were undone and she had spread the material apart, she lowered her head to his chest, covering it with the warmth of her lips. With leisurely swipes, she nuzzled his hair-matted chest with her nose and allowed her tongue to pet the muscular bulge surrounding his male nipples. When she licked at one nipple, he moaned, deep and low.

"You're already driving me crazy, woman." He buried his hands in her hair, loosening the silvery blond strands.

While she gave her mouth free rein to fondle his upper body, she moved her hands to his belt and quickly unbuckled it. With one swift jerk, she unzipped his trousers.

"You have a magnificent body." She moved her lips over the ugly, puckered scar marring the smoothness of his abdomen. "I wish my kisses could erase this scar. I wish my love could undo what Bubba's knife did to you."

"Oh, baby," he said, his voice a gruff whisper as he grasped her head and maneuvered her lips against his arousal. Only the thin barrier of his briefs separated her from his manhood.

She eased his trousers downward until they rested at his feet. He kicked them aside and stood perfectly still while Bonnie Jean ran her hands and lips down the front of his thighs. While her mouth played with his knees, she reached up and slipped her fingers inside the waistband of his briefs. "I want you naked," she said, and pulled his one remaining garment down and off.

Her lips touched him tentatively, learning the smell and taste of him, the pure masculinity of C.J. Moody.

"Baby, don't. I can't...can't stand much more." He reached down and lifted her to her feet.

They stared at each other, their hearts beating wildly, their breaths unsteady.

"Please, C.J. Let me pleasure you." She clutched his shoulders and kissed his neck, her tongue making moist circles on his skin.

"Only if you will allow me to pleasure you, too."

"Later." She began the assault all over again, working her way downward.

She took him in her hand, cradling his strength, stroking him with a loving touch. "You're mine," she said. "I love you." Her mouth replaced her hand. Consumed with passion, she pleasured him, and his pleasure became her own.

He undressed her with unsteady hands. In his haste to rid her of her clothing, he forgot all pretense of gentleness. With an almost tender savagery, he stripped her naked and lowered her to the floor in front of the fireplace.

"You make me crazy, honey," he said, his body braced above hers. "But you know that, don't you?"

When she reached out to touch him, he captured her hands and held them above her head. "My turn."

"C.J.?"

"I want you wild for me. I want to see you on fire." He lowered his head to her breast. His tongue drew circles around the nipple. Teasing her. Eliciting a cry of desire from her parted lips.

"Please. Take me now." She arched up against him. "I'm already on fire."

He ran his hand over her stomach and down to the apex between her thighs. He slipped his fingers into her welcoming warmth. "You're hot all right, but I want you hotter."

His fingers massaged her while his mouth suckled at her breast. She writhed beneath him, moaning in a frenzy of need. "Now. Please. Now."

"You want me, don't you?" He rubbed himself against her, but denied her the very thing she craved.

"Yes. More than anything." She bucked up, her body begging for his.

"Tell me. I want to hear the words."

She moaned when she felt him against her, his breath warm on her breast. "You were the first," she whispered breathlessly. "I want you to be the last."

He thrust into her with a fury that startled them both. His big body moved in a rhythm of complete possession. With each forceful movement of his body, he claimed her, erasing forever the touch of any other man. "There has never been anyone else for either of us."

In a celebration of life, Bonnie Jean and C.J. loved each other. Joy and desire blended with such subtlety that when fulfillment came it was only the beginning of their mating. Ecstasy after ecstasy shuddered through them as they gave and took until their bodies lay spent and completely sated.

Outside, the sun shone brightly and the world greeted a new year. Family gatherings. Televised bowl games. Fireworks. Black-eyed peas.

But in an upstairs room at Sugar Hill, Bonnie Jean Harland slept in the arms of the man she loved, all thought of the future banished by the security of love.

Eleven

The January sun was high in the sky when Bonnie Jean and C.J. unlocked the back door to her house on Sugar Hill. The first day of the year was half over by the time they had showered, dressed and sat down to eat a very late breakfast.

Bonnie Jean set a second plate of pancakes in front of C.J. and poured them both a third cup of coffee. Sipping the piping hot liquid, she leaned back and watched C.J. The shower and shave gave him a fresh, clean look, but still wearing his slightly wrinkled evening clothes gave him the appearance of the morning after.

She loved this man with all her heart and soul. There had never been anyone else. She had spent eighteen years without him, and now they had a second chance. But would she risk losing him again if she told him the truth about their child? What if she didn't tell him? Would it matter if he never knew?

C.J. reached across the table and took her hand in his. "You're looking very serious."

"Just thinking. Remembering."

He turned her hand over and ran his thumb across her palm. "Hey, no more sad thoughts. This is a brand-new year and we have a new lease on life."

"We can't go on ignoring the past." She pulled her hand out of his and scooted her chair away from the table. "There are things that happened years ago that have made us who we are today. We both went through so much when we were apart."

He stood up and moved around the table. With gentle pressure, he took her by the shoulders and lifted her to her feet. "I know we can't pretend the past didn't happen. Neither one of us will ever be able to forget. But why should we rehash things? I'm happier than I've been in years—maybe ever. I feel like my old self. Like that wild, fun-loving boy who fell in love with Bonnie Jean Vickers and didn't give a damn what anybody thought."

When he took her in his arms, she allowed herself the pleasure, knowing it might be the last time she knew such happiness. "Please, don't let anything change the way you feel right now."

"Hey, pretty lady, don't you know that nothing can change the way I feel about you? All those years when I thought I hated you, a part of me still cared."

She clung to him, knowing that the time for truth had come. She loved him far too much to keep her secret any longer. "I never stopped loving you. Not ever. And I love you now, more than I ever thought possible.''

''I need a little more time, Bonnie Jean.'' He held her away from him, his gaze searching her face, seeking understanding. ''I'm beginning to fall in love with you all over again, but part of me is afraid.''

''I know.'' She, too, was afraid. ''There's something I have to tell you, something about us.''

''Whatever it is, you can tell me.'' He eased her down in the high-back chair and squatted on his knees in front of her. ''I realize now that I never appreciated what we had back then when we were kids. Maybe we both had to go through hell to learn what a rare and precious thing we shared.''

''If only we hadn't been such fools!'' She pulled her knees together and hunched her shoulders, her whole body curling up in a protective move. She entwined her fingers in a prayerlike gesture and held them to her lips.

''Don't take all the blame on yourself.'' He placed his big hands on the outside of her thighs, stroking her, soothing her with comforting pats. ''What happened was more my fault than yours. Not once did I take your feelings into consideration. I never realized how vulnerable you were to pressure from my mother and from yours. I didn't really understand how inferior you felt, how insecure you were.''

''I wanted to tell you.'' She reached out and took his face in her hands, her fingers caressing his cheeks. ''But I was so afraid you'd stop loving me, that you'd realize what I really was. I didn't want you to think of me as some trashy little tramp like my mother.''

"At the time, I didn't think I compared you to your mother, but I did. If I had trusted you, really trusted you, I wouldn't have believed you capable of betraying me. I would have had sense enough to have seen through Mother's little plan."

"You honestly mean that, don't you?" She sat, stunned, her fingers trembling as they fell from his face.

"You seem to think we might not be able to overcome the past, to work through all the pain, but I—"

"You don't know everything." The words rushed out of her.

He looked at her, and the expression on her face worried him. There was something hidden in her soul, a dark secret that frightened her. "Then tell me."

"You may not understand. You may hate me again." She lowered her head, her chin resting on her chest.

"Is it about Bubba?"

"No. It's about my daughter."

Whatever it was, he didn't want to hear it. He didn't want to know anything about the child she'd had with Bubba Harland. Through all the years of jealousy and anger and hatred, the worst moments had come when he'd learned about the child. "What about your daughter?"

Oh, dear God, where did she begin? How did she tell him? "She was so beautiful, and I loved her more than anything on earth."

Pain, hot and searing, ripped through him. She had loved Bubba Harland's child. "It must have been very difficult for you when you lost her."

"I thought I'd lose my mind." It came back to her, as clear and agonizing as if it had happened yesterday. "Elaine wasn't quite twelve, but she was my life-saver. She kept me sane. I…I had to take care of her. She depended on me."

"What about Bubba? Didn't he help you?" C.J. stood up and walked around the room, restless with pain—his own and Bonnie Jean's.

"Bubba wasn't there when Cara Jean died. He was never there." Bonnie Jean hugged herself in an effort to control the tremors racking her body. "He was off somewhere with his musician friends playing gigs in out-of-the-way honky-tonks."

"Cara Jean?" The child's name played over and over in his mind like the words to some familiar melody. Cara Jean. Cara Jean. Carter. Jean. Dear Lord, had she named her child after him? After the two of them?

"She was eighteen months old. Pretty. Smart. She was walking and talking. She was putting sentences together." Bonnie Jean continued babbling, unaware that C.J. kept repeating the child's name over and over and was staring at her as if he'd never seen her before. "She could say 'Horsie go to town.' That's because I used to rock her on my knee and recite the rhyme about… She had a cold. Just a cold."

"Why did you name her Cara Jean?" C.J. asked.

Bonnie Jean looked up at him and saw the question in his eyes, the hint of realization. "I named her after us."

"Why?" He grabbed her by the shoulders and

jerked her onto her feet. "Why would you name Bubba Harland's daughter after me?"

"You already know the answer."

"Tell me." He shook her several times, then held her shoulders tightly, his pale blue eyes pleading with her for the truth.

"She wasn't Bubba's daughter. Cara Jean was yours."

"She was mine?" C.J. relaxed his hold, running his hands down her arms to loosely grasp her wrists.

"I didn't know I was pregnant when…" She couldn't bring herself to look at him, to see the pain and disgust in his eyes. "When I found out, you had already left town. I…I went to Dorothea and begged her to give me a phone number, an address. But she wouldn't. She said you had taken a job with a New York newspaper and were already on an assignment overseas."

"Did you tell Mother you were pregnant?"

"Yes." She reached for him, but he escaped her trembling fingers.

Blind fury raged inside him. C.J. grabbed the rim of the sink, his hands clutching as he bent over. "All these years, she's known? And Uncle Wheeler?"

"No. Please, don't blame them. Your mother…Wheeler, they didn't believe the child was yours. They…they thought I'd gotten pregnant by Bubba and was going to use the child to trap you."

"You married Bubba because you were pregnant with my baby and had no way of getting in touch with me?" The truth was almost more than he could bear. Knowing his family's part in forcing Bonnie

Jean into a loveless marriage. Realizing that a daughter he'd never known was lost to him forever. Admitting to himself that he was glad, yes glad, the child had been his.

"Bubba and I made a deal." Bonnie Jean walked over and placed her hand on C.J.'s back. She felt him stiffen. "He and I and Elaine and the baby would be a family. Unfortunately things didn't work out that way. Bubba knew I didn't love him, and…and I couldn't sleep with him. He never touched me until after Cara Jean was born."

"Did he mistreat you…or the child?"

"No, not at first, and never physically."

"Tell me."

"In his own way Bubba loved me, and it hurt him that I couldn't love him back. He knew I never… never forgot you."

"And my daughter? How did he feel about my daughter?"

"He pretty much ignored her, and it didn't matter because he was hardly ever home."

C.J. turned around and faced Bonnie Jean. They stood in the small kitchen, bright sunshine pouring in the windows, and stared at each other. She wanted and needed his comfort, but didn't dare ask for it. More than anything, she longed for the strength of his arms about her.

"What happened to her?" he asked. "How did she die?"

Now he'll hate me, Bonnie Jean thought. *When I tell him that Cara Jean's death was my fault, he won't be able to forgive me, just as I've never been able to forgive myself.*

"She'd had a cold and I'd been giving her Tylenol and an over-the-counter children's cough medicine." Bonnie Jean walked away, moving slowly toward the door. She looked outside to the back porch, but saw only the memories swarming in her mind. "I worked part-time as a waitress, and a neighbor watched Elaine and Cara Jean. Bubba would leave for weeks at a time, and we wouldn't have enough money to buy groceries. I…I couldn't afford a doctor."

"Damn!" The thought of Bonnie Jean and his daughter alone and hungry and in need tormented him as nothing ever had. All that Yancey-Moody money, and his own child had done without the necessities of life.

"Her cold got worse, and I finally took her to the free clinic." Bonnie Jean laid her forehead against the cool glass pane in the door. "It was my fault. I should have taken her sooner. But…but I thought it was just a cold. I had to borrow the money from another waitress at work just to buy the Tylenol and cough medicine."

"Did…Cara Jean…" Saying her name hurt him. A mental, emotional torture. "Did Cara Jean have pneumonia?"

"The free clinic was so…there were so many patients, so many sick children. They put us on a waiting list."

He wanted to hold Bonnie Jean, to put his arms around her and give her the comfort she so obviously needed. But he couldn't bring himself to touch her.

No matter how desperately he wanted to share her pain, he couldn't. Not yet. He had his own pain to deal with first.

"Finally the doctor examined her." Bonnie Jean felt oddly light-headed. The memories of that day and the days that had followed lived inside her, a daily ache that would never go away. "She was burning up with fever by the time he saw her. He had her rushed to the hospital."

"What was wrong with her?"

"Meningitis."

"How…how long did she live after…"

"They put her on antibiotics immediately, but…it was too late. I'd waited too long before taking her to the clinic. I…I let her die." Bonnie Jean turned around, her vision clear, no tears blurring her sight. She took a deep breath and looked directly into C.J.'s questioning eyes. "It's my fault that she died, and you have every right to hate me."

When he simply stood there staring at her, she wanted him to scream at her, to vent his anger and frustration, to tell her that he'd never forgive her. Anything would be better than that cold, accusatory look in his eyes.

"Why didn't you tell me? You've been back in Tuscumbia for four years. You've known how to get in touch with me for longer than that. You should have told me about Cara Jean years ago." He felt a renewed sense of betrayal—different and yet just as agonizing as what he'd felt eighteen years ago when he'd thought the woman he loved had played him for a fool.

"Would you have believed me?" She stared back at him and saw the truth in his eyes.

"No, I wouldn't have believed you."

He slipped his coat off the back of the kitchen chair, threw it over his arm and walked toward Bonnie Jean. He hesitated momentarily, gazing down at her stricken face before walking past her and out the door.

Stunned, she watched him leave. She had known he'd hate her, that he'd walk away and never come back. It was what she deserved. She'd made so many mistakes, and although she had already paid dearly, it seemed she hadn't paid enough. This time, she wouldn't get another chance.

The crisp afternoon wind turned cold as the sun began its descent on the western horizon. A clear blue sky surrounded Bonnie Jean as she stood alone in the Oakwood Cemetery. In the distance she could hear the sound of traffic, the occasional bang of New Year's Day fireworks, and the playful shouts of children. Nearby, winter birds chirped, leaves rustled in the breeze and squirrels scurried from tree to tree.

She stuck her cold hands into the pockets of her coat and stepped back and away from Cara Jean's grave. Such a tiny little grave. It had rained the day of the funeral. She had remained at the cemetery until Bubba had forced her to leave. She had longed for C.J. that day, more than any day in the two years they'd been apart, more than any day since. But C.J. had been in Southeast Asia on assignment and knew no more about his daughter's death than he had known of her life.

Rationally Bonnie Jean knew that she was not responsible for Cara Jean's death, that circumstances beyond her control had sealed the child's fate even before her birth. But on an emotional level, Bonnie Jean had never been able to forgive herself for not getting the child to a doctor sooner, for not knowing how seriously ill her baby girl really was.

She had hated Dorothea Moody and Wheeler Yancey and even her own mother. Blaming them for her misfortune had made it somehow easier to endure. But as time passed and old wounds began to heal, she realized that although all of them had played a part in destroying her happiness with C.J., she and C.J. too were at fault. Her insecurities. His smug self-assurance. Her feelings of inferiority. His lack of trust.

But nothing could change the past, and no one could give her back the child she'd lost. Cara Jean. Even now, all Bonnie Jean had to do was close her eyes and she could see her daughter. Round and plump and pink. With black curls and pale blue eyes. Her father's daughter in every way. Beautiful. Bright. Almost too perfect.

C.J. must hate her now. She would never forget the look on his face when he'd walked past her and out the back door. Out of her life forever. They had come so close to capturing the brass ring this time. They had almost made it. With Dorothea and Wheeler in their corner, they could have found the happiness they'd lost eighteen years ago, but one little secret had destroyed their second chance at love.

Tears collected in her eyes and cascaded down her cheeks. She stepped forward and knelt by her child's grave. With trembling fingers, she caressed the cold pink marble of the tiny headstone. Wheeler Yancey had paid for the monument, that fancy heart-shaped monument with cherubs engraved on each side. The date of birth and date of death were carved below the only other two words on the stone. Cara Jean.

And that was who the child had been. Simply Cara Jean. Not Cara Jean Harland or Cara Jean Vickers or Cara Jean Moody. A child conceived in love, whose birth had given her mother hope for the future and whose death had destroyed a part of Bonnie Jean forever.

C.J. turned into one of the narrow lanes leading through Oakwood Cemetery. He'd been searching for Bonnie Jean for hours, and finally sought her in a place he didn't want to go. For the past few hours he'd been driving around trying to come to terms with what Bonnie Jean had told him. They had had a child together. A daughter. And the child had died with meningitis when she'd been eighteen months old. The child whose brief existence had tormented him when he'd thought she belonged to Bubba Harland tore at his heart in a way he'd never known. He ached with emptiness.

Fierce hatred had consumed him at first. He had wanted to confront his mother and uncle, demand a retribution from them. But he finally realized that they had both paid dearly for what they'd done. In their own self-righteous ways, his mother and uncle had thought they were protecting him. And, after all these years, they regretted their mistakes enough to actually play matchmaker for him and Bonnie Jean.

In the past few months, his whole life had been turned upside down. Bonnie Jean had done that to him. She'd made him angry. She'd made him happy. She'd made him curse and laugh. The narrow-minded, embittered man he'd become over the years didn't exist any longer. A woman he had badly misjudged and treated unfairly taught him how to love again. And he did love Bonnie Jean Harland—more than life itself.

He had to find her and make her understand why he'd walked away from her earlier today. No doubt she thought he blamed her for their child's death. Dear God, he had to help her erase that burden of guilt from her heart.

Driving slowly along the unpaved lane, C.J. spotted Bonnie Jean's car parked off to the side. He pulled his Mercedes in beside her old Cadillac and stepped out. He saw her then, kneeling beside their daughter's grave, and even though he was several yards away, he could hear her crying.

Taking several tentative steps, C.J. crossed the lane. The closer he got, the faster he walked until he was running. He knelt down beside Bonnie Jean and pulled her to her feet. She swung around, startled by his presence.

"C.J.?"

He wiped away her tears with his fingertips. She

stood staring at him, dazed by his tender ministrations. C.J. took her in his arms and held her, stroking her back and whispering her name over and over again.

"I wish I'd had the chance to know our daughter." When sobs racked her body, Bonnie Jean clung to him and he tightened his hold.

"She was so much like you. Just looking at her was like looking at a little female replica of you."

"You mustn't blame yourself for what happened," he told her, turning her around so they both faced Cara Jean's monument. "I know you were a good mother and did everything you could have done for her."

Bonnie Jean leaned against him, drawing strength from his nearness. "I should have gotten her to the doctor sooner."

"That wasn't your fault." He put his arm around her waist and leaned down to place a kiss on her forehead. "I won't allow you to go on feeling guilty."

"What are you saying?" She looked up at him, disbelief in her damp hazel eyes.

C.J. fixed his gaze on his daughter's tiny grave. After reading the words engraved on the monument, he turned to Bonnie Jean. "I want to have her last name cut into that stone."

"What?"

"She was my child. She deserves my name. Even if I couldn't give it to her when she was alive, I can give it to her now." Hot salty tears filled C.J.'s eyes and streamed down his face, several droplets catching in his thick mustache.

Bonnie Jean grabbed him and hugged him fiercely as tears of grief and joy overwhelmed her. "C.J. Moody, I love you."

"And I love you, my beautiful Bonnie Jean. I love you more now than I ever did."

"But I don't want a big wedding," Bonnie Jean said, turning over in bed. She propped her arm on her pillow, bent her elbow and rested her head in her palm while she looked at C.J.

He laughed and ran the tip of his index finger down the hollow between her naked breasts. "We'll have to have a big wedding. Mother will insist. Besides, you don't want to deprive the community of an event they'll be talking about for years."

"Oh, Lord. I can hear the tongues wagging now." Bonnie Jean ran her fingers through the swirls of thick hair covering C.J.'s chest. "Can you believe that Bonnie Jean Vickers finally landed Carter Moody? Poor Dorothea must be heartbroken. And to flaunt their marriage in everyone's face by having a big church wedding!"

He silenced her rambling with a kiss. She succumbed instantly, falling into his arms, her slender body resting atop his muscular frame.

"I'd rather we elope tonight, but I think you deserve a wedding. An extravagant affair with all the social elite in Alabama attending." He took her hips in his big hands and maneuvered her so that their bodies aligned perfectly. "I want to show off my bride."

"Have I told you that I love you?" She ran a series of moist kisses across his chest and down to his abdomen.

"A few thousand times. But you can tell me again." He lifted her slightly and leisurely slipped inside her. "Better yet, you can show me."

"It will be my pleasure." She moaned when his lips touched her nipple, sipping, stroking, playing.

"No, it will be our pleasure." Every ounce of his concentration was directed to bringing the woman atop him to the pinnacle of human enjoyment.

While his mouth moved back and forth from breast to breast, he ran his hands over her hips and down her thighs, caressing, building the sensual excitement within himself. He gave her free rein and she took it. Raising herself to a sitting position, she became intent on giving and receiving the ultimate satisfaction. Her legs straddled him, her knees biting into the soft mattress, her spine arched and her head thrown back in triumph.

He reached out and took her breasts in his hands, squeezing with a gentle torture. As she accelerated her pace, he grabbed her hips and helped her set a mutual rhythm.

He groaned as she moved up and down, back and forth, creating a honeyed friction that had them both gasping for air.

"Yes," she cried out, increasing the pace to a frenzy when she felt the climactic pull inside her body. "Harder. More. More."

"Sooo…good." His voice was a low, guttural whisper.

And then fulfillment claimed her, racking her body with spasm after spasm of sizzling release. While she shook with the aftershocks of unbearable pleasure, C.J. surged up and into her with one final thrust that sent him over the edge. His big body trembled with the force of his climax. Complete and utter satisfaction claimed them both as they held each other closely, caressing, kissing, sharing words of love and forever.

"I want another child with you," he said, taking her chin in his hand and looking into her eyes.

"Yes."

"This time, I'll be with you through it all. We'll share every moment."

"Every moment," she said, then yawned and closed her eyes.

"I love you." He kissed her cheek, and reached down to pull the covers up over them.

"I love you, too," she mumbled, and dozed off to sleep. And for the first time in many years, her night was undisturbed by dreams of the past.

Epilogue

"I tell you, gal, this place looks like a florist shop," Wheeler Yancey said, glancing around Bonnie Jean's hospital room. "Flowers everywhere. Blue ribbons tied on every thing and balloons floatin' on the ceiling."

"Oh, hush, Brother," Dorothea said, her gaze focused solely on the child she held in her arms. "You're the one who sent half the balloons and flowers.'

"So what if I did?" Wheeler stood at Bonnie Jean's bedside and looked down adoringly at the tiny bundle she held in her arms. "It's not every day a man has a great-nephew named after him. Besides, you probably sent more flowers than I did."

Dorothea smiled, but still didn't remove her gaze

from the infant she held. "Well, it isn't every day a woman becomes a grandmother for the first time."

Carrying a bundle of gaily wrapped gifts, and with overflowing shopping bags hanging from his arms, C.J. Moody walked through the door.

"Good heavens, C.J., what is all that?" Bonnie Jean asked.

"They're Christmas presents for you and our sons." C.J. set the bags on the floor and began laying the presents at the foot of Bonnie Jean's bed. "Since the three of you have to spend Christmas day in the hospital, I decided to bring Santa here."

As if on cue, a round, jolly, red-suited Saint Nick bounced into the room, a video camera in his hand.

Bonnie Jean laughed and raised her head for C.J.'s kiss. After kissing his wife, he leaned down and kissed the top of his son's head. "I want to make sure we have a tape of Jack and Yancey's first Christmas."

After the four adults unwrapped the babies' gifts, C.J. lifted the two-day-old Wheeler Yancey Moody into his arms and handed him to his great-uncle. "You and Mother baby-sit while Bonnie Jean opens her gifts."

Wheeler had never known such a feeling as the one that came over him the moment he took his little namesake into his arms. When he had enlisted Thea's cooperation over a year ago, he had prayed that the good Lord would help them in their plan to reunite Bonnie Jean and C.J. After all, he and Thea had been instrumental in destroying C.J.'s happiness so many years ago.

Wheeler went over and sat down in a chair beside

his sister. "Jack there might be the oldest by a few minutes, but I think Yancey here is bigger."

"Nonsense," Dorothea said, cuddling her grandson. "They're practically the same size. Yancey might be just a mite heavier. He weighed six pounds three ounces to Jack's six pounds."

"It amazed me how a gal no bigger than Bonnie Jean carried around such a big load." Wheeler smoothed the silky blond strands atop the baby's head and looked across the room to where Bonnie Jean lay nestled in C.J.'s arms, her head resting on his shoulder.

"They're so happy." Dorothea sniffed, her eyes wet with tears. "If ever two people were made for each other…"

"Yeah, things have worked out right well, Thea old gal." Wheeler leaned over and kissed his sister on the cheek. "Bonnie Jean and C.J. have got each other and a fine pair of sons. You and I have got a clear conscience and the added bonus of seeing another generation of Yancey-Moodys enter this world."

Simultaneously Carter Jackson Moody V and his twin brother Wheeler Yancey Moody opened their pale blue eyes and let out hearty cries.

"Nothing wrong with their lungs," Wheeler said.

"Of course not." Dorothea held Jack up on her shoulder. "These young gentlemen are Moodys and have Yancey and Fenner blood flowing through their veins."

"So they do. So they do." Wheeler imitated his sister's move, placing Yancey on his shoulder.

"And having Bonnie Jean for a mother gives them a head start in life," Dorothea said.

"How's that, Thea?"

"She's smart enough to allow her sons to live their own lives and make their own decisions. She will be a far better mother than I have been."

"Well, you've got a chance now to be a good grandmother, something neither one of us thought would happen."

Dorothea looked over at her son and his wife and said a silent prayer of thanks. "Bonnie Jean, you've given me the best Christmas present I've ever had. Thank you, my dear."

"You're quite welcome, Thea." Bonnie Jean smiled at her husband, and he hugged her with a gentle fierceness.

"I'll bet when you told Bonnie Jean last Christmas that she could give you two gifts this year you never dreamed it would be twin grandsons," C.J. said.

"Never." Dorothea's smile was bittersweet. Quickly she banished all thoughts of the past. "I'd given up hope of ever having a grandchild. And now, after all this time, I have two."

*   *   *   *   *

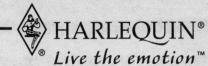

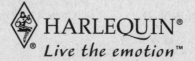

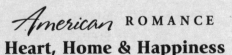
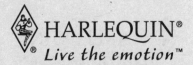

HARLEQUIN®
INTRIGUE®

BREATHTAKING ROMANTIC SUSPENSE

Shared dangers and passions lead to electrifying
romance and heart-stopping suspense!

Every month, you'll meet six new heroes
who are guaranteed to make your spine tingle
and your pulse pound. With them you'll enter
into the exciting world of Harlequin Intrigue—
where your life is on the line
and so is your heart!

THAT'S INTRIGUE—
ROMANTIC SUSPENSE
AT ITS BEST!

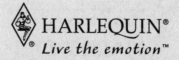

HARLEQUIN®
Live the emotion™

www.eHarlequin.com   INTDIR06

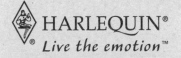

HARLEQUIN®
Presents®

The world's bestselling romance series...
The series that brings you your favorite authors,
month after month:

Helen Bianchin...Emma Darcy
Lynne Graham...Penny Jordan
Miranda Lee...Sandra Marton
Anne Mather...Carole Mortimer
Susan Napier...Michelle Reid

and many more uniquely talented authors!

Wealthy, powerful, gorgeous men...
Women who have feelings just like your own...
The stories you love, set in exotic, glamorous locations...

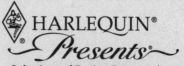

HARLEQUIN®
Presents®

Seduction and Passion Guaranteed!